"You want to scream? Go ahead. No one will hear you out here," he said, as if daring her to.

"I would if it would help," she shot back. "Can't see how that'll make it easier to be around you, though."

"*I'm* the problem?" He almost sounded sincere, but damn—that grin! It was sexy, she had to give him that, but a little sexy—okay, a lot sexy—wasn't about to make her cave. Besides, she was getting whiplash from his mood swings. One minute his hands were all over her. And then the next he couldn't put enough distance or a bigger wall between them.

"Glad you see this from my point of view," she said, knowing full well his was a question, not a statement.

The smile faded from his lips and his hand flew behind his back. "Get down."

She dropped to all fours at the exact same time his gun came around and leveled at a spot where her head had been seconds before.

DELIVERING JUSTICE

USA TODAY Bestselling Author

BARB HAN

HARLEQUIN INTRIGUE®

This book is dedicated to: Allison Lyons for making every single book better. Jill Marsal for always being there and ready to answer every question.

The great loves of my life: Brandon, Jacob and Tori, the best people I could ever hope to have in my world (I feel crazy blessed!).

Patricia Allsbrook for the last-minute save (thank you, thank you!) and always being such a steady, calming force. And her daughter, Paulina, for her quick wit (what are you, a twenty-year-old?) and warm smile.

And Babe for *always* being the one I can't wait to talk to every night.

ISBN-13: 978-0-373-74982-9

Delivering Justice

Copyright © 2016 by Barb Han

PLEASE RECYCLE
THIS PRODUCT IS RECYCLABLE

Recycling programs for this product may not exist in your area.

HARLEQUIN®

Printed in U.S.A.

www.Harlequin.com

USA TODAY bestselling author **Barb Han** lives in north Texas with her very own hero-worthy husband, three beautiful children, a spunky golden retriever/standard poodle mix and too many books in her to-read pile. In her downtime, she plays video games and spends much of her time on or around a basketball court. She loves interacting with readers and is grateful for their support. You can reach her at barbhan.com.

Books by Barb Han

Harlequin Intrigue

Cattlemen Crime Club

Stockyard Snatching
Delivering Justice

Mason Ridge

Texas Prey
Texas Takedown
Texas Hunt
Texan's Baby

The Campbells of Creek Bend

Witness Protection
Gut Instinct
Hard Target

Rancher Rescue

Harlequin Intrigue Noir

Atomic Beauty

CAST OF CHARACTERS

Jessica Davis—Stepping in for her sister puts her directly in the line of fire. When she turns up on a handsome cowboy's ranch, she realizes that she's in over her head in more ways than one.

Tyler O'Brien—He's the level-headed brother, a born negotiator. The third of six boys, Tyler is used to talking his way out of trouble. But he might have met his match with Jessica.

Jennifer Davis—This twin has a knack for getting herself in sticky situations. Her latest foray into trouble might just be her last.

Tommy Johnson—The sheriff who grew up at the O'Brien ranch and considers them family.

James Milton—This guy shoots off more lies than common sense should allow. But does he really know what happened to Jennifer?

Emma-Kate Brasseux—She owns the priceless Infinity Sapphire necklace that goes missing.

Ashton Brasseux—Does Emma-Kate's husband know more about the missing necklace than he's admitting?

Elijah Wolffe—This musician might be playing more than Zydeco. He's supposed to be Jennifer's friend. What does he really know about her disappearance?

Randall Beauchamp—Just how deeply involved is this wealthy Louisiana man and known criminal?

Chapter One

For a few seconds as Tyler O'Brien scaled Diablo's Rock and pushed up onto its crest, everything in the world was peaceful. Looking out onto the land that breathed life into his soul, he couldn't imagine a better place to be.

Tyler's gaze swept down and he muttered a curse as he stared at an overturned four-wheel ATV with an unmoving body splayed out underneath.

A dead body was not part of Tyler's lunch plans.

Tyler hated accidents. He and his five brothers had inherited the cattle ranch two months ago after his parents had died in an "accident." New evidence had the sheriff opening a homicide investigation before the will was out of probate.

"You okay?" he shouted, wishing for a response but not really expecting one. Not with the way the body was pinned under the ATV. It was too far away to get a good visual on the person. Yet Tyler had seen enough scenes like this one to get a good feel for how it would turn out.

Cell phone coverage was nonexistent on this part of the ranch so he couldn't call for an ambulance or the sheriff. He'd left his walkie-talkie with Digby, his gelding. Most ranchers used ATVs and pickup trucks for convenience when checking the vast amount of fencing on a ranch the size of The Cattlemen Crime Club. But Tyler figured his horse needed the exercise and it made him feel connected to the land to do things the way his father had. His ranch hands used ATVs, and for a split second he feared one of them might be below, but the area around Diablo's Rock was Tyler's to check.

Maybe someone had their wires crossed. Or a group of thrill seekers had wandered onto the land and one got separated.

His pulse kicked into high gear as he moved into action, digging the heels of his boots into the rocky forty-foot drop one careful step at a time. He scanned the horizon looking for the rest of the ATV party. There was no sign of anyone else as far as the naked eye could see.

Diablo's Rock wasn't a good area for people new to ATVs and only an idiot would come out here alone. There were black bears and copperhead snakes, badgers and all manner of wildlife running around this part of Texas. The land was beautiful and its danger only enhanced Tyler's respect for it. It was a reminder that people weren't always at the top of the food chain. An unprepared person could end up at the wrong end.

The closer Tyler descended toward the body, the more his pulse spiked. He could tell that the figure was smaller than a man, and that definitely ruled out one of his employees.

As he approached, he could clearly see the creamy skin of long legs, which meant the woman either had on shorts or a dress. He assumed shorts considering the fact that she wore running shoes. Neither outfit was appropriate this time of year, which struck Tyler as odd if she'd been planning on this excursion. Wouldn't she dress for the occasion? Thanksgiving was right around the corner. The average temperature in November was in the sixties in this part of Texas and this week had been colder than usual, barely breaking fifty with a blanket of cloud coverage most days.

A good part of the reason he'd intended to eat lunch on the rock was that the sun had finally broken through and its heat would reflect on the surface, offering a warm place to eat.

Then again, maybe the visitor hadn't planned on being out there at all. When Tyler got closer, maybe he'd recognize her face. The notion she could be someone he knew pricked his throat as if he'd swallowed a cactus.

People wandered off trails and did all kinds of random things while on scheduled hunting expeditions, but there was nothing on the calendar and the safety record on their land was unblemished. Right up until now, he thought.

The ATV had flipped over and was on top of her. At first blush, she looked trapped. He shoved thoughts that she could be a young runaway or in trouble to the back of his mind while he moved around the ATV, trying to get a better look at her positioning.

Her body was positioned awkwardly and close to the handlebars, but she wasn't being pinned by them as he'd first suspected.

On closer appraisal, the ATV wasn't touching her at all. And that was the first positive sign he'd had so far. He couldn't tell how bad the damage was to her body from this angle and he didn't see any signs of her breathing.

As soon as he rounded the side of the vehicle, he noticed blood splattered on the rocks next to her head. He was no expert at analyzing an accident scene but he'd heard enough stories around the campfire from their family friend

Sheriff Tommy Johnson to know the splatter most likely came from an injury to her head. An impact hard enough to create that amount of blood wasn't good.

She was facedown in the dirt with her head angled toward the side he was standing on. Not that he could see past that thick red mane of hers.

This didn't look good at all. He'd make the short hike back to Digby in order to use his walkie-talkie to call for someone to pick her up. And it was such a shame that a young woman's life had been cut short.

"We'll get you out of here soon," Tyler said softly, dropping to his knees to get a better look at her face. She wasn't wearing a backpack nor did she have a purse. A physical description might help the sheriff identify her.

Tyler brushed her hair away from her face, expecting to see her eyes fixed, and then checked her neck for a pulse. She blinked seagreen eyes instead and mouthed the words, *Help me.*

She was alive?

Shocked, Tyler nearly fell backward. His pulse pounded even faster as he located hers on her wrist, which was strong.

"You're okay. I'm going to get you out of here." Tyler had enough training and experience to know better than to move her. He needed to reposition the ATV so he could better assess her injuries.

Just as he pushed up to his feet, her arm moved and then her leg. Was she trying to climb out from under the machine?

"Hold still, there," he said. "Let me get this out of the way."

Tyler dropped his backpack and hoisted the ATV upright and away from her body. It popped up onto all four wheels. His right shoulder pinched at the movement, the old injury liked to remind him of the reason he didn't have a pro baseball career anymore, and he rubbed the sore spot trying to increase blood flow.

The mystery woman had managed to roll onto her side and was trying to climb away.

"I'm not going to hurt you so you don't have to go anywhere," he said. "I have water. Are you thirsty?"

She nodded. Based on her pallor and the freshness of the blood on the rocks, she couldn't have been out there for long. That was the second good sign so far.

He had medical supplies in his saddlebag, enough to dress a field wound. He could tend to that gash and try to stem the bleeding while they waited for help to arrive. It wouldn't take long to scale Diablo's Rock, get to his horse and then return with provisions. But he didn't like the thought of leaving her alone.

"What's your name?" He went down on a knee next to his backpack, pulled a bottle of water out of the main compartment and unscrewed the cap before offering her the bottle. He shrugged out of his denim jacket, draping it over her.

She looked like she was drawing a blank in the name department as she took the water and poured the liquid over her lips. They were pink, which was a good sign. She couldn't have been out there for long.

It didn't surprise him that she'd temporarily forgotten her name and other details about her life, given the blow she'd taken to her head. Tyler had witnessed plenty of concussions out on the baseball field. The good news here was that she could recover, a huge relief considering he'd started the afternoon thinking he would be reporting a body.

"Do you have ID?" he asked.

She looked panicked and disoriented.

"Mind if I check in your pockets?"

She shook her head, angling the bottle to get more water into her mouth than her last attempt. Again she failed miserably.

He scooted closer to her.

At this distance, he could see the dirt on her clothes. The cotton long-sleeved shirt was a deep shade of green that highlighted her lighter-colored eyes.

"Let me help you." He cradled the base of her neck with his right hand, ignoring the spark of electricity shooting through him. He shouldn't be feeling attracted to her. A sexual current couldn't be more inappropriate under the circumstances. He didn't care how beautiful she was. And she was beautiful, with her sea-green eyes, creamy complexion and heart-shaped mouth. He'd force himself to look away from her lips if it didn't mean that he'd spill water all over her face.

But feeling a real attraction to a woman he'd found lying helpless on his land a few minutes ago?

Nice one, O'Brien.

When she signaled that she'd had enough to drink, he set the bottle within her reach and then pushed up to his feet. "Okay, I'll just check for that ID, okay?"

She nodded her agreement and winced with the movement.

"Did you come out here with anyone?" he asked, chalking his physical reaction up to his overreactive protective instincts.

Looking startled, she glanced around.

Then she shook her head. Another fact she might be fuzzy on, given that hit she'd taken to her forehead.

"A group?" he continued.

The only thing he knew for certain was that she wasn't from around Bluff. It was dangerous for tourists to get lost on a massive ranch like his. She was darn lucky he—and not a black bear or hungry coyote—had found her.

She squinted her eyes. A raging headache was one of the side effects of a concussion. Luckily, that could be dealt with by popping a few pain relievers. Tyler had those in his pack, too, but the doctor would want him to wait to give them to her.

Tyler didn't want to notice her full hips or sweet round bottom as he checked her back pockets.

If he could think of another way to search her front pockets, he'd be game. As it was, he had to slip his fingers into them and ignore the way her stomach quivered.

It was safe to say that she had no ID. For the moment, neither of them knew who she was. Maybe her handbag or backpack had gone flying when she'd crashed. He scanned the ground, taking a few steps in one direction and then another.

No cell phone or purse could be seen anywhere and that struck him as odd. Tyler couldn't think of one woman he knew who would go anywhere without her cell. And that fact put a few more questions in his mind that he didn't have answers to. Like, if she was alone why wouldn't she have supplies or ID?

The panic in her eyes didn't help matters, either. Of course, waking up to a stranger and not being able to remember who she was or where she'd been would cause a certain level of panic in any normal person. Hers bothered him and he wished there was more that he could do to put her at ease.

He pushed his feelings aside as just needing to offer comfort to a stranger. It couldn't be anything more than that. He'd only known her for ten minutes, and when it came right down to it, he still didn't know her. He didn't even know her name.

"I'm going to send for help," he said.

Her eyes pleaded, filled with more of that panic he didn't like seeing, but she didn't argue. Then again, she hadn't said anything except "help me" since he'd found her.

"It's okay. I'm coming right back. I promise," he added to ease her concern. He whistled, hoping the family's chocolate lab, Denali, was somewhere within earshot. He could keep her company. After a few seconds of quiet and no Denali, Tyler said, "My horse is tied up on the other side of that rock and I need to get there so I can contact my men and send for medical attention."

She didn't relax but she nodded, wincing again at the movement. That was going to be one helluva headache when the dust settled.

As Tyler got to his feet, he scanned the area for any signs of wildlife. In her weakened state, he doubted she could fight off a flea. He pulled out his pocket knife anyway and her hand met his faster than he'd thought possible for hers to move.

"It's okay, I'm here to help."

She nodded as she took the knife.

"I'll be back in a few minutes." He filed her reaction away as another interesting thought. If she'd come out alone, what was she really afraid of? Him? Animals? She'd come out by herself without identification or a way to defend herself. This patch of land wasn't anywhere near a road. Clearly, he'd never met the woman before but he didn't have to know her to realize that she didn't look the type to wander off on her own on a four-wheeler. Not that she looked weak or like she couldn't handle herself in most situations. But the type of clothes and shoes she wore didn't fit with the activity and those expensive running shoes belonged out here about as much as a woman wearing a light jacket in the cold.

She didn't give the impression that she was a bandana-wearing thrill seeker. Nor did she particularly strike him as a granola-eating nature girl. Especially since the latter wouldn't be in the driver's seat of a four-wheeler.

There was another thing that bugged him as he walked away from the accident. He'd noticed another set of tire tracks when he scanned the ground for her personal belongings, which meant there could have been another person involved.

If she and a friend had ventured onto his land by mistake, what kind of jerk would leave her alone in her condition?

Then again, with no cell service the other person might've been forced to go for help.

And it wasn't like Red was talking. All she'd said so far was, "Help me." Pretty much anyone in her situation would say the same thing.

Tyler quickened his pace. If there was someone on his land searching for reception, he needed to get a search team out while there was still plenty of daylight. The accident might've already been called in. If the person wasn't familiar with the area he or she might not be able to lead rescuers to Red.

Even so, a person would have to be new

at this to panic and leave an injured person alone with all the dangerous wildlife here on the ranch. A darker side of him also noted that this would be the perfect way to cover up an attempted murder.

Tyler wrote the sentiment off as the result of learning that his parents had been murdered. He would like nothing more than to solve the case that had been made to look like an accident. Thinking about it made him angry. Who would want to hurt his family?

He shelved those thoughts for now.

Another one struck him about the mystery woman. If the scene back there had been an attempted murder, then the murderer could still be around. With her lying there vulnerable and alone, it wouldn't take much to finish the job.

Tyler crested Diablo's Rock and took the back side just as fast shivering in the cold breeze. He'd tied Digby to a tree in a spot where his horse could decide if he wanted to be in the shade or not.

The gelding was standing in the sun, right where Tyler had left him. He blew out a breath as he pulled his walkie-talkie out of his saddlebag and got hold of his foreman, Russ.

"What can I do for you, boss?" Russ asked.

"There's been a four-wheeler incident at the base of Diablo's Rock. A woman took a pretty bad hit to her head. She's not going anywhere without help."

"You don't know who she is?" Russ asked. It was more statement than question.

"Never seen her before. She doesn't have any ID on her and I'd put money on the fact she has a concussion."

"Sounds like a mess," Russ agreed. "Hold on for one second, boss."

Tyler would never get used to the title even though he owned just as much of the ranch as his brothers. Together, they had a ninety-five percent interest—or would as soon as the will was out of probate, which would take another ten months. The other five percent had been divided between Pop's only living brother and sister a few years ago. Uncle Ezra and Aunt Bea didn't agree on much of anything except being taken care of. The two of them were as alike as a water moccasin and a frog.

Pop had included them both in ownership of the ranch to help take care of them financially as they aged, since Bea's daughter had left for California and Ezra's only son had died before his tenth birthday. The family cattle ranch was the biggest in Texas, both in land and net profit. As if that wasn't enough, the hunting club brought in more money than they could spend, much to the benefit of the many charities their mother had loved—a tradition Tyler and his brothers had every intention of continuing in her honor.

Even though the family had money and the boys had grown up knowing that they stood to inherit the highly successful family business, none had relied on that inheritance. All six O'Brien brothers had a deep-seated need to make their own way and depend on themselves. None were like their aunt or uncle, who seemed content to ride their successful brother's coattails. Especially Uncle Ezra, who had been angling to sell his interest or be given more control over the hunting club in recent months. Tyler's older brother Dallas figured the man was getting bored in his old age and wanted more to keep him busy.

Tyler hoped that was all there was to it, especially since it was his job to keep the peace. Of all the sons, he was the best negotiator and he'd talked Ezra down for the time being. They'd already set aside one percent of theirs for Janis, their housekeeper, who would be wealthy enough not to work for the rest of her life. Although, she'd said she was way too young to retire.

"I have emergency personnel on their way to the Rock," Russ said, interrupting Tyler's heavy thoughts—thoughts he'd volunteered to ride fences to try to stem in the first place.

Ranch hands called Tyler a Renaissance man for doing things the old-fashioned way, but the truth was that it was as good for Tyler's soul as it was for Digby's health. Being out on the land on his horse made him feel connected and whole in a way he couldn't easily explain, nor did he care to examine.

"Let Tommy know about this, will you? Someone might be sick with worry looking for her," he said. The sheriff had been Dallas O'Brien's best friend and like a brother to the rest of the O'Brien boys. He'd grown up on the land. His uncle, Chill Johnson, had worked for Pop as long as Tyler could remember. Tommy had come to live with his uncle after his parents died.

"Will do, boss. I'll see if the sheriff can meet you at the hospital to take statements. Maybe he can help figure out who she is." Russ knew Tyler well enough to realize that he wouldn't be able to walk away until he knew the mystery woman was all right.

Silence meant Russ was taking care of that phone call right now, which was good because if someone had already reported her missing, then Tyler might be able to bring back more than medical supplies. He might be able to give her an identity. And if that second set of tire tracks had someone frantically searching for help, Tyler could ease that burden, as well.

"Sheriff said no one called in an emergency or missing person's report," Russ said.

Tyler feared as much.

"Said he'll meet her at the hospital since he's tied up on another interview right now," Russ continued.

If no one was looking for her, then Tyler had to consider other possibilities for those tire tracks.

"Much appreciated," he said to Russ. "Have someone ready to take Digby from me so I can head to the hospital as soon as I get back to the barn. And send out a search team in the chopper to make sure there's no one out here lost."

Tyler thanked Russ before ending the transmission and starting the journey back toward the redheaded mystery. He couldn't completely ignore the fear that he'd return to a lifeless body. She'd been upright and responsive so he'd take those as positive signs. Being away from her while she was vulnerable had his blood pressure spiking faster than a pro volleyball player. He picked up his pace, needing to see for himself that she was still okay.

At the faster speed, he crested Diablo's Rock in half the time. Part of him wondered if she could have managed to crawl away. She'd seemed determined and half-scared out of her wits—a combination that could be dangerous—or deadly—and left him wondering what really had her so freaked out.

He found her right where he'd left her. His pulse had slowly wound back to a decent clip when he saw that she was still conscious. And yet something else he couldn't quite put his finger on was eating away at him. What was the creepy, fire-ants-crawling-on-his-spine feeling about anyway?

Danger, for one thing, in the form of poachers. Sure, there were poachers in South Central Texas. People looked for trophies and illegally hunted on the large ranches in the area, which created a dangerous situation for all involved.

The O'Briens worked diligently to keep the land free of people who trespassed to hunt or steal game, so that risk should be minimal. If it wasn't poachers, then what was it? The fact that so many things didn't add up?

A beautiful single woman alone on a four-wheeler in territory she didn't know and wasn't dressed for? Yep. That made about as much sense as a deer eating barbeque.

"Help is on the way," he said, trying to give her hope to hold on to, wishing he could do more. He knelt next to her and opened his medical supply kit.

"Thank you," she managed to get out.

"My apologies if this hurts." It was going to hurt. That gash on her forehead was deep and had him worried. He poured clean water over it and then dabbed antibiotic ointment onto an oversize gauze bandage, pressing it to her forehead to stem the bleeding. She seemed determined not to give in to the pain. Or maybe she was just too weak.

It didn't take long for the cavalry to arrive. Tyler heard the chopper moving toward them before he got a visual on it. A helicopter was the only logical choice for rescue workers to use in order to access this part of the land. Otherwise, they'd have to take her on one helluva bumpy ride to get her to a main road, and that could jeopardize her condition.

Tyler saw the chopper moments before the pilot landed.

From there, it was only twenty yards to reach him and Red. The land was flat enough to manage easily on foot.

As emergency personnel neared, the mystery woman squeezed Tyler's hand.

He glanced at her and saw that same look of fear in her eyes. What was that all about? Didn't she realize this was the help she needed?

Depending on how bad that blow to the head was, she might not recognize them as the people who would help her. That had Tyler more worried than when he'd found her. Just how badly injured was she?

The blow she'd taken to the head looked bad. He'd give anyone that. But her panic looked like she was in one of those horror flicks being chased by an ax murderer.

"It's okay. I know these men. They'll take care of you," he tried to reassure her. Tyler had known the EMTs, Andy and Shanks, for years. They were good guys. Dougherty would be piloting the chopper. Tyler didn't need to see him to know that.

So what was up with the way she kept squeezing his hand, looking like she was trying to say something?

Chapter Two

The heel of Tyler's boots clicked against the white tile floor in the hospital hallway as he neared room 367 to check on Red.

He removed his gray Stetson before crossing the threshold, pausing long enough to finger comb his hair and chew on the facts. No one had reported the mystery redhead as missing or reported the accident. That had not been the news he was expecting and it made him worry that some other outsider was on his property, hurt, lost or just a damned fool who was hunting illegally and ditched the redhead when her ATV overturned. Something he couldn't quite put his finger on had his radar on full alert and it was more than just finding her in the condition he had.

Tyler pushed open the door at Bluff General and walked inside Red's room. Her eyes were closed. The bed had been raised so that she was halfway sitting and she had an IV attached to her left arm. He'd seen enough of the inside of hospital rooms to know the IV most likely contained fluids and possibly antibiotics to stem infection. All good things that her body needed to recover.

In fact, the fluids seemed to be working magic already because there was a rosy hue in the creamy complexion on her cheeks now. Her forehead had a proper bandage on it and his makeshift head wrap had been replaced with clean, white gauze.

Since she looked to be resting peacefully and he didn't want to disturb her, he figured this would be a good time to visit with her doctor and find Tommy to see if he'd managed to get a statement or put a name to Sleeping Beauty here.

Her eyes fluttered open and he felt like a fool for staring at her.

"How are you?" he asked, for lack of anything better to say. Even through the gauze and tape she was stunning.

"Better," she managed to squeak out. Her throat sounded scratchy. It was the dry air.

He set his cowboy hat down on the chair and moved next to her bed. Now that she seemed able to speak, maybe he could find out if there

were others on his land or if he should call off
the search.

"What's your name?" he asked.

She made a move to speak but coughed instead. Her gaze locked onto a large white mug
situated on the wheeled table next to her bed
just out of reach.

"You thirsty?" he asked as he moved to the
mug.

"Yes, please" came out on a croak.

At least she was talking and making sense.
Those were good signs.

"Were you alone earlier?" he asked as he
held the oversize mug filled with ice water
toward her. She eagerly accepted but didn't
answer.

After a few small sips, she leaned her head
against the pillow, but her eyes never left Tyler's face. Those sea-green eyes stayed fixed
on him, panic and fear still there.

"Do you know who you are?" he asked, setting the mug down on the tray and then re-
positioning it so that she could reach water
whenever she wanted.

"Jennifer," she said, throat still scratchy but
sounding much better. Her voice had a nice
pitch to it. "Who are you?"

"Tyler O'Brien. My brothers and I own the
land you were on earlier."

Her gaze darted toward the door and then her eyes widened in fear, so Tyler turned to follow her line of sight.

A decent-looking man in his early thirties walked in. His gaze ricocheted between Jennifer and Tyler. He was several inches shorter, so Tyler guessed he was around five foot eleven. He was on the thin side, built like a runner, and had sandy-blond hair. A fresh-looking pink sunburn dotted his tanned nose and cheeks.

Tyler didn't recognize him.

"Honey," the man said with a sigh and he seemed to pour on the drama if anyone asked Tyler. "I've been so worried about you."

Tyler glanced at Jennifer in time to see a moment of sheer panic, so he stepped in between them, blocking Tan Face's path.

"Name's Tyler." He stuck out his hand.

"What happened to you, honey? Are you all right?" Tan Face said, sidestepping Tyler and his hand.

"Hold on there, pal," Tyler said, placing his hand on Tan Face's shoulder, ensuring he couldn't get to Jennifer's bedside. "I didn't catch your name."

"James Milton," he said, puffing out his chest like a cobra, looking none too thrilled that Tyler had put a hand on him.

"Do you mind?" he asked. "My fiancée is lying in a hospital bed and she's none of your business."

Fiancée? Tyler didn't normally misjudge situations. His instincts were usually spot-on. Red seemed scared of the man. But if the two of them were engaged then he needed to take a step back. Some lines shouldn't be crossed no matter how irritated the man's presence made Tyler.

He let go of the man's shoulder. It might be better to take a wait-and-see approach to this one. Tyler told himself that he'd leave as soon as he knew she was going to be fine. Besides, he needed to make sure she had no intention of suing him for having an accident on his land. As crazy as that sounded, he'd heard of people doing that and more.

He ignored the little voice that said he was lying to himself about why he was sticking around and that it had to do with an attraction.

Milton made a dramatic scene of rushing to Red's side once he was free of Tyler's grasp. The man was fresh-from-a-shower clean and had on dress slacks and a button-down shirt. Not exactly the kind of clothes one would wear on an ATV adventure, so the logical question was why would he let Red go alone if he cared about her as much as he professed?

"I didn't know what to think when you disappeared," Milton said to her.

Tyler folded his arms and leaned against the wall. The panicked expression on Jennifer's face intensified. He'd probably regret this later, but he had to ask, "About that, James. What happened exactly?"

"I'm fine," Red interjected, her gaze darting from Tyler to Milton.

Tyler didn't have a strong reading on the guy other than general dislike and her reaction wasn't helping. Milton's concern came off as insincere. Tyler had learned long ago to trust his instincts. This guy looked like he was putting on a show.

The door opened and the sheriff walked in.

Milton turned and the look on his face when he caught sight of the sheriff was priceless. Also, it strengthened Tyler's intuition that this guy was up to no good. This was about to get interesting.

Tommy introduced himself to Jennifer and Milton, and then shook Tyler's outstretched hand.

"I've been worried sick about you, darling," Milton said, turning to Jennifer, and Tyler thought the man was overselling.

She managed a weak smile.

Tyler noticed that she stiffened when Milton took her by the hand. Not exactly a warm reception for her fiancé, and that got Tyler's mind spinning with scenarios, none he liked.

"Do you have ID?" Tommy asked.

"Did we do something wrong, sheriff?" Milton produced two Louisiana driver's licenses. His and Jennifer's.

"Just routine under the circumstances in which—" Tommy glanced at one of the plastic-covered cards "—Ms. Davidson was found."

When Tommy took down the information and then returned the cards, Milton refocused on Jennifer.

"I can't believe I almost lost you," he said, his voice had more syrup than Granny's pancakes when she'd started losing her sight but refused to wear glasses.

If anyone asked Tyler's opinion, and Tommy would as soon as they were alone, he'd say the guy was a fake. That didn't exactly make him a criminal.

"Mr. Milton, do you and Ms. Davidson mind answering a few questions?" Tommy asked.

"Don't take this the wrong way, Sheriff, but I'd like to spend some time alone with my fiancée," Milton said.

Tyler would bet his horse Milton would. He stifled a snicker.

"But I do understand that you're just doing

your job," Milton added and Tyler was sure it was part of the concerned-fiancé act.

"Given that you seem to sympathize with my position, I hope you won't mind if I ask Ms. Davidson a question," Tommy said.

"Of course," Milton responded.

"Ma'am, would you be more comfortable giving me your statement alone?" Tommy asked. "I'd be happy to clear the room."

Milton balked at the request. Before he could puff up again, Tommy held out a warning hand.

"It's part of the job," he said to Milton. Then he turned his full attention to Jennifer. "Ma'am?"

She looked to be contemplating her answer.

"Why on earth would she want that?" Milton's cheeks turned a shade of red as he focused on Jennifer.

Her weak smile died on her lips as soon as he turned back to the sheriff and didn't that make the hair on Tyler's neck stand at attention. Was she being manipulated? Abused? Milton didn't seem to want her to speak up for herself.

Tyler ground his back teeth, thinking about a man being physical with the opposite sex.

"No, thanks," she said to Tommy.

"Were the two of you riding ATVs earlier today?" Tommy asked Milton.

"Yes, and I lost her on the trail so I left and went back to our motel to wait for her," Milton said.

Tyler's eyebrow shot up about the same time as Tommy's. Tyler also noted that she'd deliberately kept the truth from him earlier about being alone on the trail. He'd seen the tracks himself. What was she hiding?

The two of them might have gotten into a fight and it could have gotten physical. He could've taken off and then she could've chased after him before the crash.

"You decided to leave her unprotected in unfamiliar territory?" Tommy asked.

"We'd had a fight." James turned toward Jennifer with a stern look.

"I searched everywhere for her once I lost her on the trail. I figured she was mad and needed to blow off steam."

"Do you realize there are black bears in these parts of Texas?" Tommy asked, incredulous.

"No. I didn't. I would never…" Milton let that sentence hang in the air. "I searched for her everywhere and couldn't find her so, like I said, I decided to give myself time to cool off, as well. I went back to my room, got worried, and when she didn't answer her cell I called around local hospitals."

"But not the police station?" Tommy asked.

Milton shook his head.

"Did you take off before or after she'd been in an accident?" Tyler asked, since he hadn't had a chance to brief Tommy on the situation yet.

Milton whirled on Tyler.

"What's that supposed to mean?" he asked.

"I was just wondering if you knew she'd been in an accident before you took off to 'cool down' as you said," Tyler elaborated.

"If I'd known anything had happened, I'd have stayed with her," Milton shot back, turning his attention to Jennifer with another over-exaggerated look.

That rang more warning bells.

And there was another thing bugging Tyler. If these two were engaged, wouldn't she be wearing a ring?

"You said the two of you were getting married," Tyler began. "Set a date yet?"

"We're working on it," Milton said. "Why?"

"Just checking to see how far along your plans are," Tyler said coolly.

"And why would that be any of your business?" Milton asked, not bothering to hide his disdain. He'd been reasonably respectful to Tommy since he was the law, but the man must see Tyler as an inconvenience. A lot could be said about a man who treated people poorly if he saw them as beneath him.

Tyler shrugged, his casual demeanor was clearly getting to the guy. "Thought it was customary for the woman to wear a ring."

Milton's gaze shot to Jennifer. "We haven't made it that far. I just asked her."

Tyler studied Jennifer's reaction. Her expression was blank, her eyes dead as she forced a smile.

She was doing exactly what Milton said and yet she feared the man. Had Tyler read this situation wrong? Sure, none of it was adding up and she looked less than thrilled to be around Milton, but no one was forcing her to be with the guy.

Tyler couldn't figure why anyone would stay in a bad relationship. And yet it happened all the time.

"There are two sets of tracks leading up to the accident. And one left. How do you explain that, Mr. Milton?" Tyler asked.

"I can't because I wasn't there," Milton responded.

"Is that true?" Tommy asked Jennifer.

She glanced up at Milton first, and then nodded.

If she was going to corroborate Milton's

story, then maybe Tyler needed to mind his own business. He'd tried to defend a few buddies who were in the middle of domestic fights and had learned just how quickly tempers could escalate. Tyler wasn't afraid of Milton; he could handle that jerk. But he couldn't make Red leave the guy.

If she wouldn't give him anything to work with, then he had to come at this from another angle.

"Have the two of you had any lifestyle changes lately?" Tommy asked Milton, picking up on Tyler's tension. "In preparation for the wedding?"

Milton's face scrunched up. "No."

"Haven't taken out any life insurance policies on each other? Named the other as the beneficiary?" Tommy pressed.

"No. Nothing like that." Milton's face looked ready to explode from anger. "Am I under arrest, Sheriff?"

Not yet, Tyler wanted to say.

"Can I see you in the hall for a minute?" Tyler asked Tommy.

"I was just about to suggest the same thing," Tommy said and then turned to Milton. "I'll be back as soon as I take a statement from the landowner."

The door had barely closed when Tyler

turned around and asked, "How is it that a man could, first, leave his fiancée outside in a strange place alone and, second, not call the police when she's missing for hours?"

"Good questions," Tommy said. "He's a jerk. I just don't have anything that I can charge him with. I need something solid in order to take him in."

"Did you notice how scared she looks?" Tyler asked. "Or the fact that he was so concerned about her that he decided to take a shower before he bothered to figure out where she'd gone or what might've happened to her?"

Tommy frowned, nodded. "It's not illegal, though."

"His story doesn't add up and he'll most likely run out of town the minute our backs are turned." Frustration ate at Tyler.

"You're right on both counts, but he has every right to go where he pleases for now. As far as I can tell no crime has been committed."

"He's hurting her." Tyler clenched his fists.

"Which is a shame, but not against the law unless someone witnesses it or she steps forward on her own to press charges."

"It should be." Tyler knew this guy was up to no good.

"I'll stay on him. If he so much as makes

a wrong turn while he's in town I'll question him for it," Tommy said.

"There has to be more you can do than that," Tyler said.

"We can scare him," Tommy said after thinking about it for a minute. "We better get back inside. I don't want to leave him alone with her longer than we have to."

"I have a few more questions for him," Tyler said through clenched teeth.

Tommy paused before opening the door. "Go ahead and ask everything you want. See if you can get him to mess up and admit to something. Without her willing to go against him, we have nothing otherwise."

Milton stood, rising to his full height when they reentered the room, which was still considerably less than both of the other men.

"Earlier, you said you lost your fiancée after a fight?" Tyler took up his position leaning against the wall near the doorjamb.

"She was tired and decided to turn back but I wasn't ready to go, so I told her how to find her way to our original meet-up point." Was Milton changing his story?

"I thought you said the two of you got into a fight," Tyler said.

Milton glanced down and to the right, a sure sign he was about to lie.

"That's what we fought about," he said, quickly recovering, as pleased with himself as if he'd just won the big stuffed animal at the state fair.

Clearly the man had just made another mistake. First he said he lost her, then he said that she turned back on purpose—which was it?

"You can't have it both ways, so pick one," Tyler said point-blank.

"Well, originally she said she was going to turn back, but then I got a bad feeling about her being out there alone in a place she didn't know and so I turned back to look for her, thus find her." Another satisfied smirk crossed Milton's features.

If that wasn't a sack of dung bigger than a bull, Tyler didn't know what was. Who did Milton think he was fooling?

Tyler's right hand fisted. He flexed and then forced it to relax.

"Good that you had time to clean yourself up, you know, while you were so busy being worried about your fiancée here," Tyler pressed.

Another frustrated pause.

"When I couldn't find Jennifer I figured she got angry at me for leaving her, so I decided to be ready to smooth things over when she came back to the motel," Milton said.

"Even though you couldn't find her when you went looking for her? You still assumed she'd be able to find her way back?" Tyler asked, not letting up. "And where was this meet-up point you mentioned?"

Milton didn't answer.

In all honesty, the man could walk out at any time. But then, that would leave Jennifer alone with Tyler and the sheriff. No way did James Milton want that.

"What are you doing in town, anyway?" Tyler continued.

"We came for the…nature. We wanted to get out of the city for a long weekend and de-compress before kicking our wedding plans into high gear," Milton said. "Life from here on out is going to be crazy, isn't it, honey?" Milton shot another look at Red.

"What trail were you on? Do you remember anything about it that stuck out?" Tyler asked.

"Not really." Milton shrugged.

"Was it rocky or were there trees?"

"Trees," Milton said, trying a little too hard to sound convincing.

"Which direction did you come from?" Tyler asked.

"We came from the north," Milton supplied.

Tyler didn't immediately respond.

"You sure about that?" he finally asked.

"Yeah. North, right, honey?" Milton said, glancing down at Jennifer.

She managed a weak smile and a nod.

No one got to Diablo's Rock from the north on an ATV. Tire tracks at the scene indicated the opposite. Tyler slanted a look at Tommy.

"That's impossible," Tyler said. "Tracks came from the south."

Anyone could get confused in an area they aren't familiar with, but this guy wouldn't be confused about direction because he was wearing one of those expensive compass watches.

"Guess I didn't notice." Milton shrugged. "If I'm not under arrest, then can we be finished with this conversation?" His lips flattened, indicating his patience had run out.

Well, guess what, buddy? So had Tyler's.

And they were far from done.

Chapter Three

"Where's the doctor?" Milton asked, rotating toward Jennifer and effectively turning his back on Tyler and Tommy. "How much longer do you have to stay in here?"

"In a hurry to go somewhere, Mr. Milton?" Sheriff Tommy asked, blond eyebrow arched.

"I'd like to get her home where I can take better care of her," Milton said. "It's impossible to get any rest in one of these places."

"And where is home?" Tommy asked.

"Louisiana, like on my license. You saw that earlier," Milton said. "You'd like to come home with me, wouldn't you, darling?"

There he went with that *darling* business again. Tyler wanted to vomit. Again, Milton was pouring it on a little thick.

While Tommy was finishing his interview, Tyler excused himself in order to talk to Jennifer's doctor, Dr. McConnell.

McConnell was a no-nonsense middle-aged woman who'd been working at the hospital since graduating medical school. A local, she wore jeans and boots under her white coat and she'd been a close family friend since longer than Tyler could remember.

"Is there any chance she's being abused?" he asked McConnell when he was sure they were out of earshot.

"I'm bound by oath not to respond to that question," Dr. McConnell said. "However, since you found her, I don't mind telling you that she has quite a few bruises on both of her arms."

"I'm guessing that's a yes," he said.

"She's been through a lot." McConnell frowned. "I'm not saying she's been abused, but even if she has there's no way to prove anything. And, of course, nothing can be done unless a victim is willing to talk about it or press charges."

"In theory, would you have offered that kind of help by now?" he asked.

"I would've. We're not talking about a child here, where I'd be forced to report suspected abuse and Tommy could step in," Dr. McConnell said. "I can only help patients who want it."

Tyler didn't like what he heard.

"When I see a patient with bruising like we've discussed, I'm always sure to have another conversation with her. I can promise that she'll know that there are folks who can help. I'll offer assistance, but it'll be up to her to accept," Dr. McConnell said, placing her hand on Tyler's shoulder. She had to reach up, considering she wasn't more than five foot three.

"Much obliged to you, doc," Tyler said.

"Before you go, any word on the investigation? It's been two weeks since I submitted the results from the third-party analysis of the toxicology report," she said, and he knew that she was talking about his parents. She'd been one of his mother's closest friends and he could see how much the doctor missed her in the dark circles under her eyes. The recent news that his parents had been murdered hit their friends hard, their children harder.

"Nothing so far, except that Tommy is reviewing the case file personally," he said. Tyler and his brothers benefitted the most from their parents' deaths so they'd be at the top of anyone's suspect list. There were no other leads at the time.

Dr. McConnell gave that a minute.

"Give your brothers a hug for me," she finally said.

"I will."

Walking toward Jennifer's room, Tyler's footsteps fell heavy. Even though he wanted to take James Milton out back and teach him a thing or two about why real men didn't hurt women, the reality was that there wasn't much else he could do at the hospital.

Tommy seemed to be wrapping things up by the time Tyler returned to the room. As much as it soured him to do so, Tyler shook James Milton's hand. Milton's wasn't moist or hot, indicating that he was fairly relaxed about the situation.

But should he be?

A man who hit a woman might be a practiced liar. Tyler didn't care much for people who couldn't be bothered to tell the truth. And this jerk was poised to walk right out the door and go scot-free. He hadn't violated any laws that Tommy could arrest him for. Tyler could see Tommy's frustration written all over his face.

"One last thing," Tommy said to Milton. "Did you have permission to ride on the O'Brien ranch?"

"Permission?" Milton echoed. His eyes widened when he heard the name O'Brien. Most people knew it and had a similar reaction.

"The land that you and your fiancée were riding ATVs on is owned by the O'Brien family," Tommy continued. "It's protected by a fence and No Trespassing signs are posted everywhere. I've been out hunting on that property myself. So, my question to you is, were you aware that you were breaking the law when you took your recreational vehicles on the land?"

"Well, no, we hadn't planned on being on his property. We got lost. Is that a crime?" For the first time in the interview, Milton looked like he might break a sweat.

"Being lost? No. Trespassing on someone else's land and destroying their property? Yes." Tommy turned to Tyler. "Will you be pressing charges today, Mr. O'Brien?"

Tyler might not be able to stop Jennifer from walking out of the hospital with this jerk but he could slow them down.

"As a matter of fact, I will," Tyler said, shifting his gaze to Milton. "You say that you innocently got lost, but how do I know that you weren't out on my property, illegally hunting?"

"I don't own a gun, for one," Milton shot back.

Tyler figured that Tommy could check the gun registration database all day long and not find a gun registered to James Milton. That didn't mean he wasn't carrying one anyway. There was no shortage of illegal guns on the black market and in the hands of people who had no business with them.

"I can't know that for sure. Besides, you might've ditched it when you realized you were close to getting caught. In fact, I have another scenario worth the sheriff's consideration," Tyler said.

"Care to enlighten me?" But Milton's gaze said the opposite.

"How about this? You take your fiancée here on a hunting trip on my land. We offer excursions but you don't want to pay the price. You decide to do things on your own. But then you hear someone and you know you're about to get caught. Rather than risk it, you take off, leaving your fiancée to fend for herself. You go hide in your motel room waiting for her to come back. You clean up because you don't want to risk anyone realizing you might've been outside. But here comes the problem. Your fiancée gets herself in trouble and ends up in the hospital, so you make up this wild story about the two of you fighting to cover for the fact that you were illegally hunting on my property," Tyler said, his gaze zeroed in on Milton.

"You can't be serious." Milton's gaze darted from Tyler to Tommy as he took a step back. A few more and he'd be in the corner.

"Sure I can," Tyler shot back, watching Milton's reaction.

"Can I see your hunting license, Mr. Milton?" Tommy asked.

Milton balked. "I don't have one. I've already told you that I don't even own a gun."

"Did you realize that you'd need one?" Tommy continued.

"I didn't come here to hunt. I wasn't out looking for game on his land." Milton shot daggers toward Tyler before narrowing his gaze when he looked at Tommy again. "I'll ask again. Am I under arrest?"

"If you were, we'd be having a different conversation right now, Mr. Milton. One that would include reading your Miranda rights to you. Since I haven't done that yet, you're free to go." Tommy turned toward the door. "But I have every intention of investigating Mr. O'Brien's complaint. In which case, I'm advising you not to leave town until this dispute has been resolved."

It was weak. Tyler knew enough about the law to know that, but Tommy was betting that Milton didn't realize it.

"I have no plans to go anywhere until my Jennifer is better. And then I have every intention of driving out of this town and back to Louisiana," Milton said.

"Mind if I speak to you privately, Mr. Milton?" Tommy shot a wink toward Tyler so subtle he barely caught it.

Tyler immediately caught on. He grabbed the pen and paper off the wheeled tray table and jotted down his cell number. Then, he moved to the bed next to Jennifer.

"You sure you're okay?" he asked.

She nodded, looking resolved. If she was engaged to Milton, then wouldn't she seem more comforted by his presence? Tyler figured he could rack his brain trying to solve that and other mysteries for the rest of his life and still come up short. There wasn't much else he could do or say if he stuck around. Red…Jennifer, he corrected himself, seemed intent on staying with this jerk. Just in case she changed her mind and wanted a friend, he folded up the piece of paper into a tiny square.

"You change your mind or need anything, call me." He managed to slip it under her pillow before Milton returned.

Tyler figured it might help him sleep at night, knowing he'd done everything he could.

Heck, who was he kidding? Those sea-green eyes were going to haunt him.

TYLER'S CELL BUZZED. He glanced at the clock on his nightstand. It was hours until the sun would rise. The noise should've jolted him awake but his eyes had barely closed all night thinking about Red.

He threw off the covers and walked over to the dresser where his phone sat on its charger, thinking what he really needed to clear his head was a night on the town and a stiff drink.

The number didn't look familiar but he answered anyway.

"I don't have anyone else to call. Please help me." The frail voice on the other end of the line belonged to Red.

Was she ready to talk? To get out of the relationship with Milton? To get help?

"Are you there?" she asked. Panic raised her voice a couple of octaves.

"Yes." he said. "As long as you're ready to tell me what's really going on."

"I'm sorry about before. It's just…" She paused, sounding almost too tired or scared to finish what she started to say. "If he finds out I'm talking to you, to anyone, then I'm dead."

"Seems to me that he's going to hurt you either way, Jennifer," Tyler said.

"My name isn't Jennifer. It's Jessica," she confided.

"I saw your driver's license," he said, chalking up the mistake to her head injury.

"Please, give me a chance to explain," she begged. "I'm not who I said I was. I know who I am and my name is Jessica."

Chapter Four

"Okay." The handsome cowboy paused as if he was seriously considering what Jessica had just said. "Is the license a fake?"

"No."

"Well then, I'm the one who's confused," he said, his voice gruff from sleep.

Jessica didn't know Tyler from Adam and yet his calming voice and masculine strength had her believing she could trust him. There was something about the tall cowboy that made her believe he would protect her.

Then again, it wasn't like she had a lot of options. The game had changed somewhere along the line and she hadn't expected Milton to try to kill her. He didn't even know that Jennifer had an identical twin, let alone that Jessica was posing as her sister.

"What's really going on?" Tyler asked.

How much should she tell him? *Could* she

tell him? She needed to say enough to convince him that she wasn't crazy.

"I wish I knew," she said honestly. All Jessica thought she was supposed to be doing was subbing for her party-girl sister, Jennifer, in order to give her time to fix whatever needed fixing. Since no one in Jennifer's circle knew she had an identical twin, the two figured they could pull off a switch and no one would be the wiser. "I need to contact my twin sister and I can't do that while *he's* watching my every move."

"You're a twin?" Tyler sounded surprised but not shocked.

"Yes. Sorry for lying to you earlier," she said quietly into the phone, praying she wouldn't disturb Milton, who was sleeping ten feet away from her bed. Jessica despised lies. Anyone could ask her ex-boyfriend, Brent, about that. He seemed to be an expert at manipulating the truth when they'd been together.

Jessica refocused. She'd waited all night for Milton to doze off, and this might be her only chance to reach out for help. She'd be released sometime tomorrow afternoon and if she didn't get away from Milton it would be all over. Jessica's memory was still spotty but one thing was clear. She needed to get away from that man while she was still alive and connect with her sister before he figured her out. He kept asking her where she'd hid "it." Jessica had no idea what he'd been talking about. Her sister had warned her that Milton believed she had something valuable and had said to pick a place to take him. When she'd taken him to the O'Brien ranch and told him she'd buried it nearby, he'd slammed a rock against her head.

"What are you asking me to do?" he asked in that deep raspy voice.

"Get me out of here," she whispered. She was taking a huge risk in calling the cowboy. Milton could wake at any second. She had no idea what her sister had gotten herself involved in, but it must be pretty darn bad for that man to want her dead.

"Is he there right now?" the cowboy asked.

"Yes."

Milton stirred in his sleep and Jessica panicked. She hung up the phone before he could catch her. If hospital staff didn't show up every hour or so she figured Milton would've already found a way to finish the job. The fact that his earlier attempt to kill her had been staged to look like an accident made her believe that he didn't want to be associated with a murder investigation.

If Jessica didn't figure out what was going on and find her sister, they'd both be dead. Losing contact yesterday had settled an ominous feeling over Jessica. She wasn't sure who she could trust anymore, except the rich cowboy who seemed determined to help. He sent her pulse racing for a whole other set of reasons she didn't want to examine. But she'd called him as a last-ditch effort to try to help her escape and find her sister. Was that a mistake?

Milton rolled onto his other side in the chair next to her bed, causing her pulse to race.

Jessica had no idea how long she'd been lying there, staring at the white ceiling, when a pair of nurses walked in pushing a gurney.

Milton shot straight up and rubbed his puffy eyes. "What's going on?"

The nurse shot him a warning look before checking the chart affixed to the foot of Jessica's bed. "We're taking our patient for an X-ray."

Milton stood, blocking her path to Jessica.

"At this hour?" he asked, puffing out his chest, and Jessica noticed he'd done that earlier when he tried to intimidate Tyler. It hadn't worked with the rich cowboy.

"This is a hospital, sir. We run 24/7," the nurse shot back and she didn't appear affected, either. "Now, if you'll step out of the way on your own it'll save me the trouble of calling security and having you removed from the building. We can do this any way you want. It's your call."

Jessica grinned despite trying to hold it in. Luckily, Milton's back was to her so he couldn't see her face. The man frightened her.

The nurse could see her, though, and she winked at Jessica as she brushed past him.

Between the two nurses, they detached Jessica from the monitors and hoisted her up onto the gurney.

Milton made a move to follow them into the hall, but the lead nurse put up a hand to stop him. "I don't think so, sir. No one but the patient and X-ray tech are allowed where we're taking her."

His agitation was written in the severe lines of his forehead, and his eyebrows looked like angry slash marks. Jessica worried that wouldn't bode well for her later. Then again, he'd made his intentions pretty clear.

Milton stood in the doorway, watching, as Jessica was wheeled down the hallway. She could almost feel his eyes on her and she'd never be able to shake the horror of turning to find him standing there, rock raised in the air, and then a sharp pain before everything went dark.

With him in the room, she hadn't been able to sleep a wink for fear he'd make sure she never woke. But that didn't make sense, did it? Would he be so bold as to kill her in the hospital where he could be discovered? Especially now that their situation had drawn so much attention. He'd gone to great pains to make his first attempt look like an accident. Jessica had every intention of figuring out why he wanted to kill her sister and what she'd gotten herself into by agreeing to help.

The nurses made a right turn at the nurse's station and then broke into a run. Before Jessica could manage to get a word out, they stopped. A blanket was tossed over her head as she was ushered off the gurney. Her claustrophobia kicked into high gear but she resisted the urge to fight against it, taking a deep breath instead of giving in to panic. She could only pray that the nurses could be trusted.

"DON'T SAY A WORD," Tyler said, turning the light on his phone toward Red as he took off the blanket.

"What are—"

"You asked me to help and that's what I'm doing," he said, hating how scared she sounded, looked. He expected her to argue or put up a fight. Instead, she wrapped her arms around him and buried her face in his neck.

"Thank you," she said, and he could feel her shaking.

Tyler would do whatever it took to help Red. The mystery woman stirred up all kinds of unfamiliar feelings. And seeing her in an abusive relationship dredged up all kinds of bad emotions from the past...feelings he couldn't set aside as easily as he'd like. He'd told himself that he'd agreed to help her solely based on the fact that she was a woman in need, but there was more. The best Tyler could do was let Red explain herself. He intended to get to the bottom of what was really going on.

"Can I use that phone?" she asked.

"As soon as you tell me why you're with that jerk."

Shock widened her sea-green eyes. "I'm not. We're not. It's just that everything's so complicated right now. I'm not sure how to explain."

"Start at the beginning."

"I need to get ahold of my sister first, so I can sort this out. Please."

Tyler figured he needed to buy some goodwill so he handed over his cell.

Red made a phone call and it ran straight into voice mail.

"That's not good. She should be picking up." Exasperation ran deep in her voice. She called another number.

A sleepy-sounding woman answered.

"Where's Jennifer?" Red asked.

Tyler now knew that she'd been posing as her sister. It was a trick his twin younger brothers had played on the family more than once when they were growing up. It had all been good-natured fun. But Red's life was on the line.

And then a thought dawned on him. Red wasn't in a bad relationship with Milton, her sister was. Maybe she was giving her sister time to get her bearings enough to leave the jerk. She might've been the one to deliver the message. A guy like Milton wouldn't have taken news like that lying down. Had he gotten angry, found the nearest rock and bashed her in the head?

"What do you mean she just disappeared?" There was outright panic in Red's voice now as she spoke quietly into the phone. "No. Don't call anyone. Don't tell anyone. Promise me you won't look for her."

Red's shoulders slumped forward and tears rolled down her cheeks as she ended the call. She closed her eyes as if trying to shut out the world.

"Tell me what's going on and we'll figure something out." Tyler's fingers itched to hold her but making that move was a slippery slope. "Does he know who you really are?"

"No. And I have no idea what I've actually gotten myself into," she said, pinching the bridge of her nose. "My head hurts."

"You can start by telling me what your sister's relationship to James Milton is," Tyler said.

The mention of Milton's name got her eyes open in a hurry.

"We can't talk here." She glanced around. "Where are we anyway?"

Tyler didn't like the idea of taking her out of the hospital without knowing exactly what kind of danger she was in and from whom, but he had no choice under the circumstances. Milton would be asking questions soon and wouldn't be satisfied without an answer. Tyler needed to get her away from the building. He pulled out a bundle of clothing. "Here. Put these on."

"Scrubs?" she asked, and when he nodded she turned to face the other way.

He took the cue to untie the back of her gown and had to force his gaze away from the silky skin of her shoulder as she slipped out of the cotton material. In addition to the surgical scrubs, Dr. McConnell had provided a bra and panties and shoes. He needed to call her in the morning to thank her for arranging everything on such short notice.

Luckily she'd believed the story about Red wanting out of the relationship. Since she'd planned to release her the next day, McConnell didn't see the harm in giving Red an out tonight. She'd joked that it was already morning somewhere and made him promise to let her stop by his place after rounds to check on her patient. Lying to McConnell sat sourly in Tyler's gut. He'd explain the situation when he could. His first order of business was getting Red away from Milton and to safety. Then, the two of them would have a conversation about delivering justice to Milton.

"What now?" Red said, turning around to face him.

"Put these on." He handed her a surgical mask and hair covering. "And then meet me downstairs near the ER. If he sees me he'll think something's up. I want to give us as good of a head start as I can."

She took a deep breath and he assumed it was to steel her nerves.

"Okay. Let's do this," she said.

"You go first. That way, if he's wandering around and happens to see you, I won't be far behind," Tyler said. "Once you walk out the door, make a right toward the stairs. I don't want you waiting around for an elevator. The ER is on the first floor so you'll have to make it down eight flights of stairs on your own. Can you handle it?"

She nodded and all he could see were her eyes, the green stood out even more against the light-blue face mask.

"Okay, then. Once you're down, I'll meet you at the ER bay," he said. "Don't forget to take off the mask before you walk out of the stairwell."

Red stood at the door for a long moment. She pressed her flat palm against it but stopped short of opening it.

Then she stole a last look at him before walking out and to her right.

Tyler figured he needed to wait a bit before he followed. It would take all his self-control not to hightail it to Red's room and deliver his own brand of justice. Milton needed to see what it was like to fight with a man. But that would only alert the creep to the fact that Jessica was on the run. Since Tyler couldn't be in two places at once, he waited a few minutes, then pushed the door open. If Milton saw him at all, it could be game over.

Besides, there was a lot more to this situation than met the eye and Tyler needed to get to the bottom of what was going on before he let his fists fly. He'd take Jessica to the ranch for tonight. There wasn't a place around with better security than home.

Tyler made it down the hall and then to the elevator without incident. In the ER, Red was standing right where he'd told her to and a part of him sighed in relief. He couldn't be sure that she wouldn't bolt as soon as she had the chance and he had all kinds of questions that needed answers.

Then again, she was in a strange town. Running from the one person helping her didn't make a bit of sense.

So far, Red had told Tyler that she'd stepped in for a sister who was now missing. Twins. He shook his head as he walked toward her. Wouldn't his little brothers Joshua and Ryder have a field day with this? Red and her sister's trick would be right up their alley. Even though they weren't actually identical, his youngest brothers looked enough alike that they got away with a few too many pranks, switching places to confuse people.

Tyler took Red's arm and led her out to his waiting SUV.

"What has your sister gotten herself into?" he asked as soon as they were safe inside his vehicle. He turned the key in the ignition and backed out of the parking space.

As he meandered through the lot and onto the highway he expected her to speak. She didn't.

"We can turn back and I'll ask Milton, if that makes you feel better," he threatened. No way would he go through with it but she needed a little motivation to get her talking.

"I told you before, she's my twin sister. She's in trouble."

"What kind?"

"I don't know exactly what's going on," Jessica said, staring out the front window.

"Then start with what you *do* know," he said.

"I got a call from my sister three days ago asking if I could take time off work to help her out," she said. "She needed me to step into her life and go on a trip with a friend of hers for a few days while she fixed a problem. She said go along with whatever he said, so I did. This isn't the first time I've had to bail her out of a bad situation, so I agreed."

"Is your sister involved in something illegal?"

"Before yesterday I would've been ready to fight if you asked that question about her. Now, I'm not sure what she's gotten herself into," Jessica said on a heavy sigh. "She's not a bad person. I normally get called in for a relationship that has gone south and she doesn't have the heart to break it off herself. I show up and help ease her out of it. At least that's how it started five years ago. It kind of grew from there."

"So you had no prior relationship with Milton?"

"We're not engaged, if that's what you're asking, and neither was Jenn," she said with an involuntary shiver. "I'd never seen the man before two days ago. My sister sent me with him. She said I could trust him and to go with him and pretend that I knew what he was talking about. We checked into the Bluff Motel and he started demanding that I tell him where something was. Some kind of box. I can't remember clearly." She touched the bandage on her forehead.

"Is that how you ended up on my property?"

"Yes. I picked a remote place thinking that he'd give up when we couldn't find the box right away. He got angry instead. Demanded that I tell him where it is, told me to stop playing games. I said that I'd tricked him and had no idea where the box was. The next thing I know I'm being hit in the head with a rock," she said, leaning back against the headrest. "Where are we going, by the way?"

"My ranch," he said.

"Maybe you should just take me to the airport and drop me. I can grab a flight or rent a car there and drive to Louisiana. I have to find my sister."

"In case you haven't noticed, you're in no condition to drive anywhere. Milton still has your ID so renting a car or getting on a flight is out of the question," Tyler countered. "And then there's the issue of him trying to kill you. We need to update the sheriff first thing in the morning."

"No. We can't."

Was she serious? She balked pretty darn fast when he mentioned Tommy.

"This is his town and he has a right to know the truth. You should be pressing charges against that jerk who tried to kill you," Tyler said. "In case you hadn't noticed, he seems intent on finishing the job."

"I have," she retorted, motioning toward her forehead. "But I have no idea what's really going on, I can't remember everything, and I've already put my sister in danger by leaving the hospital. All I know for sure is that Milton isn't the one in charge. Until I know who's trying to hurt her, I can't bring in the police. You can drop me off at a bus station."

She wouldn't last a day without money or

transportation, and she seemed to realize it about the same time Tyler started to tell her.

"This must look bad to an outsider," she said. "But I have to ask you to keep everything I've told you between us. Give me a little time to figure out what happened to my sister and help her."

"She might be hiding."

"Or hurt," she said.

"In which case, doesn't it make more sense to bring in the law?" Tyler turned in to the ranch and security waved him ahead.

"This isn't a good idea. I shouldn't have called you and gotten you involved," she said, and he could hear the fear and panic in her voice. Not a good combination.

She looked exhausted, and his first priority was to get her inside where she could rest.

"Let's not make any decisions tonight," Tyler said, pulling up to his two-story log-cabin-style house. Their parents had built each of the brothers a home on the expansive ranch in hopes they would someday take their rightful places at the helm. Tyler's was on the south side to take advantage of the sun. Most people hated the heat in Texas but it couldn't get hot enough for Tyler. His mom used to joke that he had to be cold-blooded because of how much he loved summer.

He'd spent most of his childhood outdoors, throwing a baseball, football or whatever was around with one or more of his brothers. His childhood had been happy and filled with loving memories, and his blood boiled at the thought that someone had wanted his parents dead. They were kind, respected members of the community. His mother had one of those hearts that had no bounds. Pop was honest, albeit stern.

Tyler pulled into his attached garage and parked his SUV.

"Hold on," he said as he slid out of the driver's seat and then rounded the vehicle to open her door for her.

"Are you hungry?" he asked, offering a hand.

"I'm more thirsty than anything," she said, putting her fingers in his.

A frisson of heat fired through his fingertips and he noticed how small and delicate her hand was by comparison. He pushed those thoughts aside. His mind was still reeling over how much he'd misjudged his last girlfriend, Lyndsey. The last thing he needed was another complication in his life. "We can fix that."

There was a noise at the front door, a scratching sound.

Tyler opened the front door and let the family's chocolate lab inside. He patted his old friend on the head and scratched him behind the ears.

"This is Denali," he said to Red.

"Is he yours?"

"Denali?" Tyler glanced up. "Nah. He belongs to everyone. He drifts to each of our houses now that we're home, and he's been known to stay in the barn from time to time."

"He's beautiful." She hesitated. "And big."

"This old boy won't hurt you," Tyler said.

She moved a few steps closer and bent down. Denali jumped up at about the same time and her cheek met a wet nose. Jessica let out a yelp before reaching to scratch Denali behind the ears.

"You hit his favorite spot. Don't be surprised if he follows you around now," Tyler said.

She smiled as he helped her into the kitchen and for the first time could see just how weary she looked. Even in an exhausted state, Red would be considered beautiful with those big eyes, thick lashes and creamy complexion.

"I have some homemade chicken soup in the fridge. How does that sound?"

"Impressive. You cook?" She eased onto a bar stool at the large granite island.

"Not me. I had some delivered from the main house."

"This ranch is amazing. Are you telling

me there's even more to it?" she asked. She glanced around the room as he divvied up the soup into two bowls and heated them in the microwave.

Tyler couldn't help but laugh. "More" was an understatement. "Each of my brothers has a house on the ranch, and then there's the big house my parents lived in. They kept one wing open for guests of the hunting club we own."

"What kind of ranch is this?"

"We raise cattle and provide hunting expeditions."

"How many brothers did you say you had?" she asked as he set a steaming bowl in front of her.

"Five. Six if you count Tommy. He spent most of his childhood here. He and my older brother Dallas have been best friends since before I can remember." He took a seat at the island next to her. "Be careful. It's a little hot."

She blew on the spoon before taking a mouthful. "Either I'm *that* starved or this tastes even better than it smells."

Denali had gone to sleep at her feet.

"Probably a little of both but Janis Everly is an amazing cook. Her soups are a whole experience in and of themselves," he said with a smile. It was true. The woman could cook. "You should see the main house during the holidays. Everything's decorated to the nines and the whole place smells like cinnamon and nutmeg. Janis cooks every kind of cookie imaginable. She dresses up like Mrs. Claus and delivers them just about everywhere in town."

"She sounds like an amazing woman," Jessica said.

"She's a saint for putting up with us all these years," he said with a laugh, liking the smile his comment put on Jessica's face as she bit back a yawn.

He showed her to one of the guest rooms after she'd drained her bowl. A few hours of rest should clear her thoughts and let her come to her senses.

Then they could get to the bottom of whatever was going on. And even though she'd protested, he had every intention of bringing in the law.

Chapter Five

The *rap, rap, rap* against the front door shot Tyler straight up out of bed and to his jeans, which were laid out across a chair next to his bed. The machine-gun-like knocks fired again. Tyler hopped on one leg trying to get his second leg in his pants and stay upright.

He shook his head like a wet dog, trying to wake up, and glanced at the clock. Almost six thirty. What on earth?

He took the stairs several at a time and saw that Tommy was standing on the other side of the door.

"What's going on?" he asked as he opened the door and motioned for the sheriff to come in.

"I'm here on official business," Tommy said, and the tone of his voice didn't sound good.

For a split second Tyler thought his friend might be bringing news about his parents, except that he would've called all the O'Brien's together first. So this had to be about Red.

"You want a cup of coffee?" Tyler asked, moving toward the kitchen.

"No, thanks. I've already been on duty for an hour." Tommy followed. "I'm here to talk to you about a murder."

Tyler stopped in his tracks and spun around. Those words had the same effect as a good, strong cup of coffee. "Let me guess. Milton's dead?"

"No. He's missing. We haven't identified the victim yet," Tommy said.

"What does this have to do with me?"

"The body was discovered at the Bluff Motel," he said with an ominous sigh. "In Jennifer and Milton's room. I have to ask. Where were you an hour ago?"

"Here. Asleep," Tyler said, and he could see that his friend didn't like asking that question.

"Have you been here all night?" Tommy asked.

Tyler's phone records would tell the story so he decided to come clean. "No. I went to the hospital to check on Red after she called and said she was ready to leave the jerk. I brought her home with me."

Tommy's eyebrow arched severely.

"What else was I supposed to do?" Tyler

asked, his shoulders and hands raised in surrender as he stood there in the kitchen in an athletic stance. "She reached out for help and I said I'd protect her. Dan Spencer was working the security gate when we came home and he can tell you that we arrived around three o'clock this morning. I fed her soup and put her up in the guest room, and that's all."

"She's here right now?"

Tyler nodded, motioning upstairs.

"Get your coffee. It's going to be a long day," Tommy said, taking a seat at the granite island.

A few minutes later Tyler joined him with a fresh mug filled with strong coffee. He took a sip. "You want me to wake her?"

"I'll need to talk to her," Tommy said.

"What happened to Milton?" Tyler asked. "He was at the hospital with her when she called asking for help."

"He must've left after you got her out of there," Tommy supplied.

Tyler took another sip, letting that information sink in. "He must've realized pretty quickly that something was up at the hospital."

"How'd you get her out of there without him knowing?" Tommy asked.

"Dr. McConnell arranged it on the condition she could check up on her at my house. She sent in a couple of nurses saying they were taking her for X-rays. I took over once they got her safely away from him." He paused long enough to take another sip. "I tried to convince Red to press assault charges a few hours ago."

"But she refused," Tommy finished. He knew the drill all too well. Except that this was no run-of-the-mill abuse case.

Tyler nodded. He'd let his friend make his own assumptions for now. But he had every intention of filling Tommy in as soon as he could.

"What happened at the motel?" Tyler asked.

"A couple in the room next door heard two men arguing, banging noises against the wall and then a few minutes later a car sped away. They didn't think much about it at the time, figured someone had too much to drink. The noise woke their baby and the husband got sent out to the car to get extra supplies from a diaper bag. When he returned he noticed the door next to his was still open. He thought it was strange and decided to check it out, make sure everyone was okay. That's when he saw a man splayed out on the floor, bleeding out. He tried to administer CPR and yelled for his wife to call 911," Tommy said.

"But it was too late," Tyler said.

Tommy nodded.

"Sounds personal," Tyler said.

"Very personal," Tommy echoed. "He stabbed him with a hotel pen, which means he grabbed anything he could find. Then he panicked and ran without thinking about closing the door behind him, which leads me to believe that he wasn't expecting the confrontation."

"Any chance this was a random mugging?" Tyler asked. Red was in more danger than she realized. If she truly was covering for her sister, and he believed her story, then Jennifer was into something very dark and dangerous. He also believed that Red had no idea what was going on and he found himself wanting to help her even more.

The truth lay somewhere between Texas and Louisiana, and Tyler had every intention of finding it.

"Nothing appears to be missing, although we won't know what happened for sure until we talk to James Milton." Tommy leaned against the counter. "If it had been a coincidence, though, he would've reported it."

"You're expecting to get the truth out of that man?" Tyler coughed.

"About as much as I'd expect a deer to drive a car. This whole scene looks like self-defense, but then Milton took off in a hurry, leaving behind his clothes, shaving cream, pretty much everything he brought with him as far as we can tell." Tommy dragged his boot across the tile floor. "And I'm left wondering why he would do that and not go straight to my office."

"Seems strange."

"Everything about Milton is off. From his fiancée ending up in the hospital and him expecting us to believe that lame story about losing her, to a man being stabbed to death in his motel room."

"What about the dead guy? Have you identified him yet?" Tyler asked, trying to absorb just how much danger Red was in. He also hated lying to Tommy, allowing him to believe that Jessica was her sister. He had every intention of clearing up the misunderstanding as soon as he spoke to Red. Tyler despised lies and they were racking up.

"No. He had ID on him but it was fake." Tommy's boot toe raked behind his other foot.

"What about transportation?"

"We're still working on the rest of the pieces." Tommy glanced up and tilted his head to the left. "We have no leads. Unless Jennifer knows what's going on."

"I can vouch for her whereabouts last night. She's been with me the whole time."

"The neighbor heard male voices. We aren't looking for a female." Tommy said. "And yet that doesn't rule out the possibility she might be able to fit the pieces together for me. Right now I have a dead stranger at the morgue with a fake ID, and a man on the run who could be anywhere or right under my nose looking for Jennifer. Based on his actions yesterday, I'd say the man doesn't want to leave town without her."

"I didn't trust or like that guy from the minute I laid eyes on him, but I'm just as confused as you are. She hasn't told me a thing since we got here." He glanced at the star-shaped metal clock in the kitchen. It was ten minutes until seven. "I'd hoped to give her a few hours of sleep before I talked some sense into her and brought her down to the station to press charges against Milton. At the time, I thought that SOB shouldn't get away with hitting women."

"That's not all he does," Tommy said on a heavy sigh. "The problem is figuring out what else he's into before I have another dead body in my town."

And if Tyler could save Red in the process that would be even better.

"It goes without saying that I'll need to speak to his fiancée to find out if he had enemies," Tommy added.

Why did the sound of the word *fiancée*

string Tyler's neck muscles tight? He nodded, feeling the tendons cord and release.

"Did the witness hear what the two were arguing about?" Tyler asked.

"He said he was half-asleep but he thinks he remembers hearing him ask something about a necklace and where the girl was," Tommy said.

"They argued about Red?" Tyler did his best to act surprised. Damn, he hated withholding information from Tommy. But the surest way to lose Red's trust would be to go behind her back by telling his friend everything he knew. Tyler feared she'd strike out on her own and end up getting herself hurt again or worse… dead. She was in so far over her head she couldn't see right from wrong anymore, and Tyler was her best bet at finding the straight and narrow again. She seemed like a good person in a crazy situation, and Tyler of all people understood her need to protect her family.

"I believe I will take you up on that cup of coffee," Tommy said.

"Help yourself," Tyler said, draining his cup and pushing to his feet. "I'll go wake her so you can talk to her."

He could take a few minutes to prep her for what was to come, he thought as he knocked on the door of the guest room. He hated the idea of waking her before she'd had solid sleep.

There was no movement on the other side so he cracked the door. "Jessica."

No answer. She must be out cold. His ringtone sounded from down the hall as he pushed open the door to her room. The bed was empty and there were no clothes to be seen. The door to the adjoining bathroom was wide open but he checked inside anyway.

Jessica was gone.

Tyler darted into his own room and answered his phone before it rolled into voice mail. The call was from Dan in security and Tyler knew right away that Jessica had hit his radar.

"What happened," Tyler asked.

"Sir, a white female is being detained in the guard shack. She was seen running across the south side of the land after exiting your house," Dan said.

Tyler needed to make a decision. Bring her in and let Tommy question her, or make an excuse and talk to her first? He opted for the second. "Take her to the main house for me and wait there with her."

"Yes, sir."

Tyler ended the call, threw on a shirt and made his way downstairs where Tommy waited in the kitchen.

"I'm afraid she's gone," he said, stuffing his cell in his pocket.

"What do you mean gone? Do I have anything to worry about with her?" Tommy asked, setting his cup of coffee on the counter.

"She's afraid and she's been traumatized. There's no way she could've been involved with the stabbing because she was with me. I know you have to handle this like every other case, so I already told you that Dan at the guard shack can corroborate our story. The only reason I didn't call you before is that she didn't want me to involve law enforcement even though I told her it was the right thing to do." Tyler hedged, hoping his excuse would hold water and Tommy would chalk her disappearance up to her being abused. "I'm sure one of the guards will see her. In the meantime, she's been through a lot and I'd like to get out and search for her myself. She doesn't exactly trust men right now."

"By all means," Tommy said. "Bring her by the station for a statement when you find her. Or give me a call and I'll come right over. Time is the enemy in a homicide investigation."

"I will," Tyler said, hoping he could convince her that Tommy was on her side. Having help from someone in law enforcement could prove beneficial.

"This mess could take a while to untangle. A man like Milton probably has a lot of enemies." Tyler grabbed his keys from the counter.

"I'd bet money on it." Tommy was already walking toward the door. "I'm heading over to the motel now. Maybe we'll know more once we process the scene."

"While I have you here, have you made any progress on your investigation into Mom and Pop?" He thought about Tommy's comment about time being the enemy of a murder investigation. Were all the leads cold on the O'Brien case?

"I'm sorry. I don't have anything new yet. You'll be the first to know when I do." Tommy excused himself and walked out the door.

Tyler grabbed a pair of socks from the downstairs laundry room and slipped into his boots. He was ready to head to the main house when someone knocked on the front door. He could see Red with Dan standing next to her.

"What happened?" he asked as soon as he opened the door.

"I'm not ready to talk to the sheriff. I decided to take a walk and this guy forced me to go with him," Jessica said, chin up in defiance. Determination filled those sea-green eyes.

"I'm sorry, sir. I tried to take her to the main house but she went ballistic," Dan said, looking exasperated. "Given her condition, I thought it was safer to bring her back to you."

"Thank you. I can take it from here," Tyler said to Dan.

"Yes, sir." Dan excused himself.

"Are you okay?" Tyler asked Jessica as soon as he closed the door behind her. He couldn't help but notice the red marks on her arms and wrists, still fresh from yesterday, as he ushered her into the kitchen. And she was shivering.

"Me, yes. At least for now. My sister is the one who is in trouble," she said, rubbing her arms to warm them.

"Pull another stunt like that and I might not be able to help you," Tyler warned, his anger raised from a place deep inside…a place that made him feel helpless and weak. He bit back a curse as he retrieved a blanket from the couch and handed it to her.

"I can't make any promises. I'll do whatever it takes to make sure my sister is safe." Jessica draped it around her shoulders before folding her arms across her chest in a defensive position.

"Come and sit down. I'll get you a cup of coffee." Tyler didn't wait for her to make a move toward the kitchen before he walked over to his counter. He poured two fresh mugs. He needed to tell her the news about what had happened back at the motel and he needed to find a way to do it without scaring the hell out of her. "You like sugar or cream?"

"Black is fine," she said, accepting the mug and taking a sip.

"You want to sit?" Tyler asked, motioning toward the bar stools at the granite island.

Red seemed to catch on to the fact that he had news. She set the cup on the counter and turned to face him, hands fisted on her hips. "What is it? What's happened?"

There was no good way to put this, so he decided to come out with it straight. "A man was found dead in your motel room."

"Milton?" Red sank to her knees. Her skin paled. Tyler crossed the room and helped her onto the stool a few feet away from her.

"No. Not him." Anger tore through him again when he realized how badly she was shaking, this time from fear not cold.

"How?" she asked, looking utterly stunned. "Who?"

"Tommy doesn't know the answer. The guy had a fake ID so they'll start trying to identify him. As for how, he was stabbed to death after arguing with a man who we suspect was Milton," Tyler said. "A witness says the two were fighting about a woman and a necklace. I'm guessing the woman is your sister and you by proxy. Any idea what the necklace is about?"

"THAT'S THE FIRST I've heard about it but maybe that's what is in the box," Jessica said. Hold on a second. Was it? A memory pricked, like a sudden burst, and then it dawned on her as she brought her hand up to the bandage on her forehead. The bump to her head must've confused her and made her forget. "My sister wanted him out of town. She needed to get him out of the way as she investigated something…I can't remember what. But she told me to go with him and agree to help him find the box. Once we got here, my sister told me she was getting close and to drag this out as long as I could."

"And that's exactly what you did," he said, and there was anger in his eyes.

"Right before I got my head smashed with a rock after telling him I'd tricked him and had no idea what he was talking about." She pulled the blanket from her shoulders and set it down.

"Feeling like he'd been duped must've made a man like Milton angry," Tyler said.

"He'd rented the ATVs and we were on your property by the time I fessed up. I remember that much. I'd stalled as long as I could. He got so frustrated his face turned red and he started demanding to know where the box was." She glanced at the bruises on her arms. "I expected him to be upset but I never thought he'd try to kill me."

Tyler's grip on the coffee mug intensified.

"He kept hinting at my neck when he talked about the box. I thought he was threatening me, you know, for show, because I never expected him to try to hurt my sister. Now I realize he must've been referring to a necklace."

Tyler's eyes widened. "I wonder…"

He retrieved his smartphone and pulled up a news story. She squinted at the screen to get a better look at the headline: Infinity Sapphire Stolen from Prominent Louisiana Family.

She quickly scanned the story. "This is the most famous necklace in America that isn't stored in a museum?"

"Seventy-seven-point-seven carats total weight," the handsome cowboy added. He stood so close that his scent filled her senses— a mix of woodsy aftershave and warmth, deep and musky—and it stirred up all kinds of inappropriate sensations.

"You know about this necklace?" She took a step back, needing to put a little space between them, and tried not to memorize his unique aroma.

"The couple that owns the necklace attended an art auction hosted by my family recently. I didn't get a chance to talk to them. I prefer to be outside when all that's going on." He paused, turning the phone over and over in his hands. "Forgive the question, but I have to ask. Is there any chance your sister's a jewel thief?"

"None. Zero. I'd bet my life on it," she said, and she pretty much already had. "Whatever's going on can be cleared up as soon as I speak to her. She might not even know how much danger she's in. I have to find her before Milton or anyone else does."

Jessica was already up, pacing, when the cowboy touched her shoulder. It was all she could do to ignore the frissons of heat zinging through her.

"We will." His honest dark eyes seemed like they could see right through her. He was gracious to help her as much as he had already, but this situation had detoured to a very bad place and she didn't feel right putting anyone else at risk.

"It's too dangerous for you to be involved. Someone is dead because of this necklace. I can't ask for your help anymore."

"Let me be the judge of that," he said quickly. "Besides, I'm not going anywhere until I know you're safe."

Looking into his eyes, she could see he meant it and she figured it was most likely some kind of cowboy code. But she couldn't let anything happen to him, and especially not since he was being so generous helping her.

She started to protest but he stopped her with that same look.

"This is the situation as I see it. You have no transportation, no purse, and you have no idea who's after you. To make matters worse, you won't go to the law. So forgive me when I say that you don't have a lot of options right now. I'm willing to help and I'm your best bet to keep you alive and find your sister." He folded his arms and spread his feet in an athletic stance. "If those are your goals, and I believe I'm correct in saying they are, then I don't see how you're in a position to refuse my help."

He was right about all of it. There was no denying what he said was true. "I do want to live and you're absolutely correct about how desperate my situation is. But I still think it's a bad idea for you to get involved any further. Milton's out there, somewhere, probably looking for me. He must think that I know more than I'm saying or that I'm getting the necklace for myself."

The cowboy's slight nod said he agreed. He

made a sound of disgust. "What exactly was his relationship to your sister?"

"All I know is that they dated a year or so ago. I thought he was out of the picture but I guess they stayed in touch. She dated society men and I'm sure it's a small circle."

"Did she mention anything specific about why she decided to leave him before?"

"There were a lot of things. Like, for instance, if a hostess said their table would be ready in twenty minutes and it wasn't, he would become and angry and didn't care who knew." She looked at Tyler whose dark eyes penetrated her poorly constructed armor. She wanted to lean on someone, on him, even temporarily. "I knew he was a creep, but Jenn didn't mention anything about him being physical with her."

"Violence can escalate." Tyler's boots scuffed across the floor as he paced. "I'm sure Tommy will run a background check on him as part of his investigation." Tyler stopped and held up his hand. "I know what you're going to say, so don't bother. But we will need to get Tommy more involved at some point."

She started to protest but he just shook his head. "I won't go behind your back, so don't worry. But we have to bring in the law. We'll talk more about that later. Right now, I want to hear more about Milton."

"Jenn said he was upstanding but she might not've known him as well as she thought she did. He is…let's see…I know she told me…oh, right. He's a lawyer."

"He didn't sound like one when Tommy interviewed him," Tyler said.

"Right. He's a corporate guy, mergers, I think."

"That explains the shiny shoes and his lack of knowledge about criminal law," Tyler quipped, walking past her and once again filling her senses with his scent.

"I don't know much else. I'm not even sure where he works but I'm guessing he's with a corporation in or near Baton Rouge where she lives." Jessica held up her coffee mug and breathed in the smell of dark-roasted beans.

"She said he was a jerk but she didn't give details?" He shot her a look of disbelief. "Sounds unusual for twins."

"I remember thinking she might've been too embarrassed to talk about him in detail, like he was seeing someone else while she thought they were exclusive or something along those lines." Jessica braided her fingers. "The relationship didn't last long. She didn't call me in to break up with him, so they might've remained friends or run in the same circles. That's about all I remember. I had no idea he was capable of actually hurting her. And now my memories are patchy about the past few days."

"Not surprising, after the hit you took to the head," he said.

"I think I'm awake enough for the day." She set down her empty mug. "Mind if I get cleaned up in the bathroom?"

He stopped pacing and stared at her for a minute. She knew exactly what he was thinking. "I'm not planning another escape, if that's what you're worried about."

His cheeks dimpled when he smiled. "There's a spare toothbrush in your bathroom. It's still in the wrapper. I'll have breakfast delivered."

She figured it would do no good arguing with a cowboy whose mind seemed made up, so she resigned herself to accepting his help.

"Tell me one thing, though," he said as she started to leave the room. "How'd you sneak out this morning? I mean, you were on the second floor and I didn't hear you leave."

"I couldn't sleep, so I heard the sheriff when he pulled in. The alarm code was easy because I watched you enter it last night. You seemed like a nice person but after being with Milton I had no plans to take that chance. I slipped out the side door."

She kept to herself how relieved she was that she hadn't gotten away for exactly the reasons he'd mentioned earlier. She was broke, alone, and had no means of communication. Not to mention the fact that she had no idea where she was and there would be all manner of wildlife outside that door. Plus, she was barefoot.

She was also desperate and she had a bad feeling about her sister's current situation. "Jenn might be trying to reach me on my cell. Can we go to the motel room and check if it's still there or is there no way now that it's a crime scene?"

"We can do whatever you want. But first, we're heading into the station so you can give a statement to one of the sheriff's deputies," he said matter-of-factly. "And if you want to stay above suspicion you'd better act like an unhappy fiancée."

Chapter Six

"Do you think he believed me?" Giving her statement to the deputy had taken Jessica all of fifteen minutes, mostly because she didn't know anything. She'd played the shocked fiancée as best she could, forcing tears that came only when she let herself think about her sister.

"You didn't give him a reason not to," Tyler said.

Jessica sank into the tan leather seat of the SUV as they drove to the motel room she'd shared with Milton. An involuntary shiver rocked her body at thinking about being in that place with him.

She should've been able to see right through that fake smile of his. Milton had charm in spades when he wanted to turn it on, and she could see why her twin would've been attracted to him. He was good-looking and had a professional job with what Jennifer would see as plenty of earning potential.

Jennifer had always wanted more out of life than the meager childhood they'd had in Shreveport. Both of their parents had worked low-wage jobs to support the family. Their mother had owned a cleaning service, her father had made a living doing seasonal yard work, and all three kids had had to pitch in to help summers. Jennifer had always imagined herself living in one of the grand Southern colonials they'd cleaned while Jessica had always been the more practical sister. She'd been able to see right through the men who dated Jennifer for superficial reasons and then dumped her when it was time to find a proper wife.

Tyler steered onto the highway. All makes and models of trucks blazed past them.

"I was remembering my last conversation with my sister. She said that she was involved in something and she needed to figure a way out, to clear things up. Or at least, I think that's what she said." Jessica gingerly fingered the wrap on her forehead.

"Which could mean that she is guilty of taking the necklace," Tyler said, and she couldn't argue with his reasoning. That's exactly what this would look like to an outsider. Except that she knew her sister better than that. Jennifer could be flighty and she definitely liked a good party and hanging out with the high-brow crowd, but she was honest.

Convincing the handsome cowboy of that was a whole different story. She couldn't prove that her sister wasn't involved. All she had to go on was how well she knew Jenn. *Twins for life!* had been their mantra since they were little girls and most of the time it felt like they could read each other's thoughts. Jessica had no such magic now and the silence was terrifying because she feared her sister was in grave danger.

"Jennifer might come off as insincere, and sometimes she is, but she's also good underneath all the layers. Freshman year she went to Houston for college. I helped her move into her dorm and we went shopping to pick up a few extra supplies. We get in the car and Jenn realizes that the clerk had forgotten to charge her for a twelve-dollar pillow. It was late August in one of the hottest summers on record in Texas. Jenn's car had no air-conditioning. But Jenn was worried that the clerk would get in trouble for the mistake. Drenched in sweat, she marched back inside to let him know."

She stared out the front window. "I consider myself an honest person, but I would've returned to pay for the pillow another day or waited until the sun went down. Not Jennifer. No amount of begging could change her mind. By the time she got back I was dripping so I made her stop off at the nearest gas station so I could buy a cup of ice to rub on my sizzling skin." And that was just one of many examples that came to mind.

Jessica could tell Tyler all day that her sister would never take something that didn't belong to her, but she had nothing concrete to prove it and he had no reason to believe her. "I can see how this looks and if I was you I'd probably assume the worst and that she was a bad person—"

"Hold on there. No one said anything about jumping to the worst-case scenario. We need to think through every possibility and I'm going to have to ask hard questions along the way. If you say your sister couldn't have stolen something then I believe you," he said. "Let's work with the assumption that she had no idea what was really going on but got herself tangled in this mess. That makes more sense anyway, because you two are close and based on my intimate knowledge of twins she wouldn't knowingly put you in danger. Someone could've used her. Even made it look like she was the one who took the necklace to cover for themselves."

"That necklace is worth a fortune. I'm betting Milton isn't the only one trying to find it, aside from my sister," she said. "With millions on the line, a lot of bad people would come out of the woodwork."

"Which could explain the man at the motel and if that's true, then I doubt Tommy will be able to identify him. He could be a treasure hunter or working for organized crime."

"One of how many?" She touched a sensitive spot on her head and winced.

"There will be a lot. Some of them will be official. Insurance companies hire interesting people to help investigate and recover merchandise like that, and a necklace worth millions would be insured to the nines," Tyler said. "And then there's the black market."

Just the thought made her head hurt even more. "And my sister is tied up right in the middle of this, of all these vultures."

"It would seem that way. Tommy is going to be following the same paths and I'm going to have to bring him in at some point," Tyler said, and she thought about it for a long moment.

"Okay. But not without discussing it with me first." She figured she could hold Tyler off long enough to get her bearings and for them to make enough progress for her to walk away and make sure he wasn't in danger. Eventually she'd have to break out on her own. "I need to speak to my sister. It's the only way to be certain of what we're dealing with. I talk to her and everything will be cleared up."

"You couldn't reach her earlier."

"True." She chewed on her bottom lip. "I need my cell. She may have left a message or a clue. I bet she's been trying to reach me and I haven't been able to answer. I hid my phone because Milton was creeping me out. That's why I didn't bring it with me when we went out on ATVs. I was afraid he'd take it and then he'd know." Jessica sat straight up in her chair, remembering a little more. "I find my cell and we get answers."

THREE-INCH-WIDE crime scene tape, Big Bird yellow with bold black lettering, stretched across the door of room 121 of the Bluff Motel. The sun was out and it was finally warming up a little.

A sickening feeling sank low in the pit of Jessica's stomach as she walked across the black asphalt toward the room she'd been forced to share with Milton. It was bad enough that a man had been killed only fifteen feet away, even a man who was after her sister or James Milton didn't deserve to be stabbed to death, but she could feel the sense of despair hanging in the air. Knowing what had happened and seeing the evidence right in front of her made everything that much more surreal. A man was dead. Her sister was missing.

Jessica's stomach clenched and she tried to stave off nausea. The sheriff ducked under the tape and moved toward them. He was holding a paper bag—evidence?—which he handed to a deputy.

"I couldn't be sorrier about what happened here," the sheriff said with a genuine look of compassion. "Has your fiancé been in touch with you?"

In the moment, she'd almost forgotten about keeping up that charade.

"No, he hasn't. But thank you very much, sheriff. This is all such a shock." That much was true. Everything about the past thirty-six hours had turned everything she knew upside down and twisted up her insides. "I'm afraid I lost my cell so I don't know if he's been trying to contact me."

Tommy nodded, which she took to mean neither he nor his deputy had found it.

"See anything in there that might help you figure out what happened?" Tyler asked, diverting the sheriff's attention, and she was grateful for that.

Jessica didn't have that same ability to fudge

the truth with people that came so easily to her sister. In her heart, her sister was a good person incapable of hurting a soul. Of course, Jennifer never would have called it lying. She'd prefer to say something like *bending the truth*.

Tears leaked from Jessica's eyes. Her sister had to be all right. If she'd gotten herself involved with men worse than Milton, Jessica was even more worried.

"I ran James Milton through the system," Tommy said to her. "How well do you know your fiancé?"

"I learned a great deal more about him recently. Why?" Jessica wasn't sure where this was going and she didn't like lying to someone in law enforcement.

"What did you find?" Tyler asked, drawing the attention to him again.

Jessica shot him a grateful look.

"He has a record," Tommy said matter-of-factly.

"For what?" Tyler asked as Jessica gasped.

Tommy looked from Tyler to her. "I'm guessing by your reaction you had no idea."

"No. I would never have even guessed." Jessica didn't have to fake her reaction. She was genuinely shocked and even more worried for her sister. If the sheriff confused her reaction for feelings for Milton so be it. "You think you know someone."

"I made a call to Baton Rouge PD and he's pretty well known for having gambling issues."

"Meaning the issue is that he loses," Tyler added.

"They don't call it a problem when they're winning," the sheriff said wryly. "He's wanted for questioning in several cases the PD is trying to clear up, everything from small cons to extortion. They booked him on a small-time charge."

"I had no idea," Jessica said honestly as she tried to digest this news. She'd discovered that her so-called fiancé was a con man who'd set her up. More questions for Jenn were mounting. Jessica wondered if Milton had heard about the necklace and decided to steal it and cash in. Maybe he had debts to pay with the wrong people and one of those could've been the man that had been killed.

"Ever hear of Randall Beauchamp?" the sheriff asked.

"He's the head of one of Louisiana's wealthiest families," Jessica said. "And I've heard that he doesn't make all his money from legitimate sources."

Had Jennifer gotten herself mixed up with one of the biggest crime families in Louisiana?

"The Baton Rouge police chief seems to think that Randall Beauchamp is on the hunt for a stolen necklace worth millions of dollars on the black—"

Before Tommy could finish his sentence, Jessica sank to her knees. Nausea threatened to overwhelm her. Her world tilted on its axis as the reality of her sister's situation set in. Jennifer was as good as dead.

Was Milton working for the Beauchamps? Maybe he was greedy and wanted to sell the necklace in order to settle a gambling debt. Or maybe he needed the money to disappear.

Bile burned the back of Jessica's throat as she felt herself being lifted up by strong arms.

"You don't have to do this right now" came Tyler's masculine tone, and it sent a warm current running through her. "We can deal with all of this later."

"It's okay," she said as he led her to the passenger seat of the SUV. She turned to face him. "I need to do this."

The sheriff stayed put. A deputy had brought over something he must've wanted to show his boss and the two were engaged in conversation.

She and Tyler were just out of earshot. "I need to find my phone."

"Tommy or one of his deputy's might already have it."

Jessica shot him a look.

"No. There's no way Tommy will release evidence in a murder investigation. He can't."

Jessica looked him dead in the eyes. "I hid it in between the mattresses."

"Hold on" was all he said and then he walked away.

THE DEPUTY WHO had been talking to Tommy put an evidence bag in his cruiser as Tommy disappeared inside the cordoned-off room.

"Hey," Tyler said to Deputy Garcia. "Mind talking her off the ledge?"

Tyler motioned toward Jessica, hating that he was about to lie to his friends again. He'd known Garcia since middle school.

"What's going on?" Garcia asked.

"She's still in shock about all this. First, she decides to leave an abusive relationship and now a man turns up dead in her fiancé's motel room. I think she's blaming herself in some weird way, like if she'd stayed with him then everything would be okay," Tyler said, praying his friend bought into the lie. "And now finding out that not only was he abusive but he was a criminal seems to have put her over the edge."

"Not sure what I can say to help but I'll try." Garcia shook Tyler's outstretched hand before walking over to Jessica.

There were only two law enforcement officials on the scene that Tyler had noticed so far. Hopefully Jessica could keep Garcia occupied while Tyler worked on Tommy.

Tyler glanced at Garcia, who had his back turned to him, and then ducked under the crime scene tape.

The room had worn dark blue carpeting and two full-size beds with heavy bedspreads that looked exactly like the curtains in his Gran's old house. Beds, perfectly made, were to the right and there was a plywood desk and a dresser made of the same quality against the wall to the left. This was the sort of place that most likely bolted the furniture to the floor and nailed pictures to the walls.

Noise came from the bathroom beyond and Tyler figured Tommy was there collecting evidence and looking for clues.

He ran his hand along the box spring of the second bed, figuring that Milton wouldn't want Jessica sleeping closest to the door in case she decided to bolt.

Bingo.

He tucked the phone in his front pocket and then turned to sneak out.

"You shouldn't be in here," Tommy said, standing in front of the closet leading to the bathroom. His arms were folded and his feet braced.

"I was just looking for you." Damn. Tyler was a bad liar.

"I'll give you a hint. I'm not in one of the drawers of the nightstand." Tommy hadn't bought the line.

"This?" Tyler turned to the nightstand with the phone and alarm clock on it, stalling for a few seconds while he tried to think up an excuse. He saw a pen and notepad with the hotel logo on it. Snatching them up, he then turned toward Tommy. "I was looking for these."

Tommy's cocked eyebrow said it all. "Don't touch anything else. I don't need your fingerprints all over my crime scene."

At least he didn't seem to realize that Tyler had shoved something inside his pocket.

"What did you want with me?" Tommy asked.

"Glad you asked. I wanted to talk to you without Red in the room. Do you think there's any chance she knew what was going on?"

That seemed to ease Tommy's concerns. "Her reactions seem genuine to me. This is catching her off guard. Why? You think there's a chance she knew?"

"Not really. I just wanted to make sure I was on the same page as you after she reached out to me," he said.

"She thinking of leaving town anytime soon?" Tommy asked.

"Good question. She hasn't mentioned having family to take care of her. We already know she's from Baton Rouge. I don't think she's in a big hurry to go home, considering Milton could be there now."

"Men who abuse women like to cut them off from the rest of their family. So, even if there is someone she might not've spoken with them in months or years," Tommy said.

Tyler clenched his back teeth. "She may have had a dust-up with her family about him."

"She'll need counseling and a lot of support. Even though Milton can't hurt her anymore she needs help dealing with her emotions." Tommy's hands had relaxed and he'd slipped them inside his pockets.

"Milton's a first-class jerk."

"My guess is that the lawyer got himself in trouble with some gambling debt and that could be responsible for the timing of their trip. He might've hoped things would cool down back home," Tommy said.

"We didn't trust him from the beginning," Tyler added.

"Nope. He's a scumbag. I'm planning to dig deeper into whether or not he had a life insurance policy on Miss Davidson. She may not have known he'd taken one out and her *accident* seems even more suspect now. An insurance payoff could clear up any debt Milton had and set him up nicely."

"Good point. I didn't like him from the get-go and I like him even less now that I know about his background. She said he was an attorney and an upstanding citizen. Guess he put on a good act," Tyler said.

"Love is blind," Tommy quipped. "I see it all the time in my line of work." He paused. "She seems like a nice person."

Tyler nodded.

"I see that you're helping her out and she needs a friend. How far do you plan to go?" Tommy asked, accusation in his tone.

"Why wouldn't I lend a hand? She needs a place to catch her breath. It's been a crazy couple of days for her. I figure I'll help her get straight, maybe get Doc McConnell in to speak to her, and then send her back to Louisiana where she belongs."

"Be careful," Tommy warned.

"Of what? Her?" Tyler blew off the comments.

"Yes. I know you, Tyler O'Brien. You're not

going to be able to turn your back on some-one who needs a hand up. This woman's been through a lot and I'm warning you as your friend not to get too involved."

A throat-clearing noise came from the door-way. Jessica stood there. "Are you ready to go now?"

Tyler nodded and shot Tommy a warning look. Although he wasn't thrilled that Jessica overheard the conversation, he was relieved that she'd given him an out. He used it to walk out the door and past the tape.

Once they were safely inside the SUV and he was sure no one could hear, he said, "I found it."

"My phone?" There was a mix of apprehen-sion and excitement in her tone. And fear.

He nodded. "We'll check it out as soon as the motel is safely in the rearview."

"Thank you," she said, adding, "and he's right, you know. A man is dead. This is dan-gerous—"

"That's not your fault," Tyler interjected.

"No, it's not. But I'm heading toward the people who killed him and that isn't safe for you." She didn't miss a beat.

"It's not for you, either. Will knowing that stop you?" he asked.

"No. My sister's in danger and I can't walk

away. I have to find her. I don't have a choice," she said impatiently.

He took his right hand off the steering wheel once he got the SUV up to speed on the highway and squeezed her left. The contact sent a jolt of electricity up his arm. "Neither do I."

Tyler managed to dig into his front pocket while keeping the wheel steady. He produced a cell and placed it in Jessica's hand.

"Now, let's see what's on this phone."

Chapter Seven

Tyler made sure no one was following them before exiting the highway. He located the closest parking lot, a Dairy Queen, pulled in and parked.

"There are three calls from my sister," Jessica said, and her face had gone bleached-sheet white.

"Put the phone on speaker," he said.

She did.

Sis, I'm so sorry that I got you involved in this mess. This is so much bigger than I imagined. I'm worried about you. Call me ASAP and get far away from James. He isn't who I thought he was. I gotta go. Call me.

Tyler shouldn't be surprised at the likeness of Jennifer's voice. After all, his twin brothers' voices were similar, too. And yet it still threw him off.

The message also confirmed what Tyler

already knew, Jessica had no idea what was going on. He'd trusted her and confirmation that he hadn't made a mistake in that trust eased a little bit of the tension cording his shoulder muscles.

"She sounds good," Jessica said, wringing her hands together. Fear, anxiety and apprehension were embedded deep in her eyes.

Are you okay, sis? You're not calling me back and I'm starting to get worried about you. If James has hurt you in any way... Click.

"What's that noise in the background?" Tyler asked. "Do you recognize any of the sounds?"

Jessica tilted her head to the left and leaned toward the speaker. "I hear zydeco music and that must mean she's with her friend. He lives in Spanish Town. That's encouraging. She'd be safe with him."

"You said there are three messages," Tyler said, holding off his warm and fuzzy feelings for now. Jennifer had already misjudged one so-called friendship but he didn't want to burst Red's bubble of hope just yet. With millions of dollars on the line, Jenn shouldn't trust anyone.

Sis, run. Jennifer sounded out of breath, like she was running, and there was the sound of splashing water in the background. There was a long pause. *Wherever you are, run. Hide until I tell you it's safe to come out. Oh, God,*

I hope you're okay. If James figured you out don't believe anything he says. I had no idea what was going on. Don't go to the police. Don't trust anyone and especially not... NO!

Jessica heard her sister scream.

...I've gotta go. I'll figure a way out of this, I promise. And then I'll meet you on the bayou.

Her words came out at a frantic pace now. Another scream came through the line and then there were sounds of a struggle. More screaming and a male voice telling her to stop kicking. He yelled a profanity and then came the sound of her phone being dropped in water.

A desperate Jessica held the phone so tightly her fingers lost color and now matched the pallor of her face. Anger quickly overrode all other emotions. She banged her fist on the dashboard. "They got her. It's the only logical reason the calls stopped."

"Do you recognize the man on the recording?" Tyler asked.

"No."

"What did she mean about the bayou?" he asked. Maybe he could nudge her out of an emotional state into logical thinking. Get her wheels turning.

"It's just a saying we have between us. Doesn't really mean anything." She turned to him, those sea-green eyes wide. "But they have her and now they'll kill her."

"Can I see that for a second?" Tyler peeled her fingers off the phone and scrolled through the call log. She was worth millions to them. They wouldn't kill her. He didn't see the need to bring up the fact that they would most likely torture her to get that information. "The last call came in while you were in the hospital."

"They got her so they no longer needed Milton," Jessica said. Good, she was using her anger to switch gears and think this through, and that was the best chance they'd have of finding Jennifer.

"That's one thought. Another is that someone else, a freelancer, has gotten in on the game. This necklace is famous and, like I said before, it's worth is going to bring people out of the woodwork to find it," he said, needing her to have a realistic picture of what they were facing and hoping he'd be able to convince her to bring Tommy up to speed. Tyler never went back on his word. He wouldn't go behind her back.

"She was at The Bluebonnet Swamp Nature Center during that last call," Jessica said.

"How do you know?"

"She's my sister and that's where she'd go if she was in trouble." Jessica's matter-of-fact tone had him convinced. "Plus, I heard her sloshing through water and there were sounds of nature all around her in the background. And I heard her slap her skin from mosquitoes a couple of times. This is the first place she'd go to hide because that's where I used to find her when she had a bad breakup with one of her boyfriends. She knows the area and probably figured it would be a good place to lay low, which also means she didn't want to involve her friends by staying with them."

"We'll start there." He handed her the phone and put the gearshift in Reverse.

"That's got to be a six-hour drive from here, at least," she said, sounding defeated. "Plus the call came in yesterday. She won't still be there, not if that jerk got to her, and I know he did. That's the only reason she wouldn't call again."

"Maybe she lost her phone. I heard the sound that it made hitting the water," he offered.

"She would've borrowed someone's to call and check in with me. We never go more than a day without talking and it's been at least twenty-four hours since her last attempt."

Tyler believed her, having witnessed the same phenomenon firsthand with Ryder and Joshua. Those two spoke daily.

"Baton Rouge is only an hour away from here by plane." He redirected the conversation. Last thing he needed was her dwelling on the negative.

Tyler made a few calls using the hands-free Bluetooth feature preloaded on his SUV and had set up their flight and itinerary by the time they reached the airstrip. He just hoped like hell they got to Jennifer first.

THE FLIGHT WENT off without a hitch and a private car waited at the airport. Jessica's stomach had braided into an unbendable knot the second she'd heard her sister's voice on the third message and it hadn't let up.

"You said before that few of her friends know about you," Tyler said, ushering her into the backseat of a stretch limousine with blacked-out windows.

"That's right."

"I'd like to keep it that way," he said. "Especially since we believe she's been taken and others may not realize that."

"I wouldn't exactly call this incognito." She waved her arm in the air.

"Sometimes, the easiest way to hide is to be in plain sight."

The limo zigged in and out of traffic terrifyingly, but then southern Louisiana drivers were notorious for fast lane changes, tailgating and high speeds. Even being from Louisiana, Jessica had a difficult time navigating traffic in and around Baton Rouge. Don't even get her started on the bridges or thoughts of the alligators that lurked beneath them.

Rain threatened and a wall of humidity hit full force as they stepped out of the limo, stealing Jessica's breath. She'd get used to it in a minute, but those first few breaths after stepping out of an air-conditioned car were always staggering.

Tyler paid their entrance fee into The Bluebonnet Swamp Nature Center.

"I promise to pay you back as soon as the sheriff releases my personal belongings," she said earnestly, thinking about everything he was doing for her and hit hard by the realization that she'd never be able to equalize this debt.

He waved her off.

"No, seriously." It was important for Jessica to feel like she could cover her own bases. That was the only thing she didn't like about her sister. It was too easy for her to flash a smile and let someone else do the work for her. And even though Jessica had that same smile, she'd always known it would get her and her sister in trouble if used improperly.

Tyler mumbled something she didn't quite catch. She'd let it go, for now. A man as good-looking and wealthy as Tyler O'Brien was most likely used to getting his way. But he hadn't seen stubborn until Jessica put her mind to something. He'd learn just how persistent she could be when this was all over and she could put her affairs back in order. For the time being, though, she had to live off his generosity if she wanted to find her sister in time.

"There must be dozens of boardwalk trails here." He stood behind the Nature Center building looking at the maze of wooden paths.

"She likes a certain place. There's a bench close to an old cypress tree. The branch is huge. They built the walkway beneath it. Follow me," Jessica pushed past him, plucking at her shirt as beads of sweat rolled down her chest even though the temperature was barely seventy.

Jenn's favorite bench was a good ten minutes' hike from the Nature Center building. At their pace, they made it in seven. "There it is."

She ducked under the cypress branch, a good three feet wide, and dashed to the bench, wanting to soak in everything from the last place she knew her sister had been.

Tyler walked to the bench and dropped to his knees to get a better look at the water.

"I hope you're not planning on going in there," she warned.

"It's not like I want to," he said. "But we might be able to locate her phone."

"We?" No way was she getting in water with snakes and alligators. Jessica involuntarily shivered. "You know what's in there, right?"

"Sure do."

"I can't help my sister if I'm in the belly of an alligator chewed up into little pieces," she said, frustrated. Because she would do anything to save her sister, including jumping into that murky green water that scared her beyond belief.

Tyler's chuckle was a deep rumble in his throat and it sent a sensual vibration skittering across her skin. She was about to be eaten by an alligator and the cowboy she'd brought with her was causing her to have inappropriate sexual thoughts.

"At least let me take my shoes off first."

"How deep do you think the water is here?" he asked.

"A few feet, four at the most."

"Look for bubbles before getting in." He was lying flat on his stomach on the boardwalk, watching the surface of the water. "I'd rather wait at least twenty minutes but we don't have that kind of time, so I want you to look hard."

Wasn't that reassuring? A serious case of the heebie-jeebies trickled down her spine as she moved to the other side of the boardwalk. Okay, she could do this. She needed to talk herself up for a minute to steel her nerves, but this was going to be no big deal. She scanned the water intently, watching for any signs of life.

"I think I should be good here," she finally said, stopping twenty feet from her original spot.

Tyler popped to his feet and moved a good ten feet from his first location. "All right, then. We're looking for her cell or anything that might indicate she was here."

He ducked through the slats in the wood and then she heard the splash that said he was in the water on the other side. Jessica took in a deep breath, held it, and then slid through the wooden slats on her side. The murky green water was cold against her stomach as she waded through waist-deep water. Moss gathered on her stomach and she nearly lost her cool. Every survival instinct inside her begged her to get out of there and run away.

Jenn needed her. The fear and desperation in her sister's voice would keep Jessica on the right path.

"Something just brushed past my leg," she said, letting out the breath she'd been holding.

"We better move quickly before someone sees us and kicks us out," Tyler said.

Jessica dropped down, trying to feel her way around in three-foot-high water. All she touched was slick rocks and she tried not to think about all the bacteria lurking around and what that would do to a cut in, say, her finger.

Every noise made her jump. Every animal sound made her heart race. Every scrape of her finger across a new surface made her pull her hand back.

After searching for what seemed like an eternity and coming up empty, she returned to the boardwalk and scrambled out of the water. She quickly checked her body for leeches or any other creepy-crawlies. "Did you find anything?"

"No." The water-sloshing sound came from the other side of the walkway.

"It's useless." And worse yet, felt hopeless. She should've known this would be a dead end.

THE ARCHITECTURE OF Spanish Town was mostly post–Civil War. Rows of early twentieth-century homes of wood construction lined the narrow streets. Houses were small but had large front porches and there was more pink in one place than Tyler had ever seen. "What's up with the flamingos on all the lawns?"

But "on the lawns" was an understatement. They hung in front windows and stood on porches. There was even one on a roof.

"People used to look down on this area as having questionable occupants, so everyone decided to give them something to stare at," Jessica said. "Mostly artists and musicians live here."

"And what do we think we'll find amongst all this plastic fowl?" he asked. Their shoes and clothes smelled like swamp. The limo driver hadn't wanted to let them back inside wet. Tyler had had to slip the guy extra money to convince him it would be a good idea. He'd also promised to pay for having the limo properly cleaned and aired out, which he figured he owed the guy.

"Jenn has a friend here. I might be able to trick him into thinking I'm her."

"The zydeco music playing in the background of the first message?" he asked.

"Yes. I'm hoping she confided in him, but she might have just wanted a place to lay low. His name is Elijah, by the way." She scanned the houses. "I'm just not sure where he lives, exactly."

"Do you think it's safe to go in like this?" he motioned toward their soaked clothing.

"Probably not, but what choice do we have?" she asked with a shrug.

"We need to play this smart. Not attract too much attention. Someone could be watching Elijah's place and we're soaked to the bone. Give me a few minutes." Tyler fished his cell from his front pocket and made a call. "Janis, can you book a room for me at the Hilton in Baton Rouge?"

"Fine but I'm putting you in the Presidential Suite," Janis said.

"Okay." Normally, he'd argue. There was no need to put him up in the best suite in any hotel. But this time, he had a lady with him and the two-bedroom suite would give her the privacy she needed. They were still practically strangers, even though it felt as if he'd known her for a lot longer than thirty-seven hours. Rather than try to get inside his head about what that meant, he requested fresh clothes in a woman's size five to six to be delivered to the hotel. And then he asked for men's. Janis already knew his sizes. "Casual stuff in a breathable fabric. Also, I'm going to need hats and maybe a few ladies' scarves. Think you can get all that to my room in the next hour?"

"Does a dog have fleas?" Janis quipped.

"Thank you, Janis. You already know I think you're the best." Tyler buzzed the driver who rolled down the partition between the cab and the backseat. "Can you take us to 201 Lafayette Street?"

"Yes, sir, Mr. O'Brien," the driver said.

"I'm going to need your services 24/7 while I'm in town," Tyler said. "Is that a problem?"

"No, sir." A smile lit the driver's face.

"Thank you. I'll double your current rate."

An even bigger smile curved the driver's lips. "You don't have to—"

Tyler put his hand up. "It would make me feel better for inconveniencing you on such short notice."

"I don't know what to say. Thank you."

"What's your name?" Tyler asked.

"Zander, sir."

"How about you call me Tyler? Every time I hear 'Mr. O'Brien' I look over my shoulder to see if my father's standing behind me."

Zander chuckled. "You're the boss, Mr.—" he glanced in the rearview with a sheepish look "—Tyler."

"Thank you, Zander." Tyler turned to Jessica. "You haven't eaten since breakfast. What sounds good?"

"Nothing, I'm okay."

"You need to keep up your strength." He placed a call to the hotel manager and arranged for soup, sandwiches and bottles of water to be waiting when they arrived. Tyler ended the call to Jessica's wide eyes.

"Can I ask a question?"

He nodded.

"I've seen your place and where you live is beautiful. There's more security than a...a... maximum security prison. So, I hope I'm not being rude, but just how rich are you?"

Tyler couldn't help but laugh. He never really thought of himself as wealthy. Rich in land and family, maybe, but not rich in the loads-of-money-in-the-bank rich. Maybe it was the way he'd been brought up. Pop had had his feet firmly planted in the soil and all the boys had followed suit. They cared more about running their horses—speaking of which, Digby needed exercising—than running up credit cards. But by all measures, they were loaded. "Guess I never think about it."

"How can you not?" she asked, eyes wide. "When I first met you I thought you were some kind of ranch hand, which was fine by me. You seem so...normal. But now I see that you own your own plane and can fly it rather nicely, by the way. You can snap your fingers and have almost anything you want delivered or arranged...am I on the right path here?"

"Not everything," he said. "And nothing that really matters."

"Tell me one thing you can't make appear?"

"My parents." He didn't miss a beat. "No amount of money can bring them back. We're about to have the first Thanksgiving without them, without Mom's cooked goose and all the trimmings, and it feels odd. She was all the warmth in the holidays. Her meals. Her traditions that me and my brothers used to think were corny as kids. That's the stuff you miss, the little things. The way she used to make these maple cookies in the shape of leaves and the whole house smelled like pancakes and cinnamon. Now all I can think is how my own kids won't ever bake pies or cut out paper snowflakes with her."

"I'm so sorry." Jessica touched his arm, and it was as though her words reached into his chest and filled some of the emptiness in his heart. He'd heard those three words more times than he could count in recent months and yet this was the first time they'd had healing power.

"Your mother sounds like an amazing woman," she said.

Tyler nodded, fearing that if he said any more he'd get choked up. Next thing he knew, Jessica had braided their fingers together.

"There's no way to replace the people we love and no amount of money can fill that void.

My sister has essentially turned her back on us trying to do just that—make a bank account somehow fulfill her life. I never understood that about her. I love her with all my heart, don't get me wrong, and money's nice. Living without it stinks. But just like that old saying goes, it can't buy love. It's refreshing to hear that your family has it right."

Tyler agreed. "Being close with my brothers helps, having their support makes losing our parents easier to get through. This first holiday will be hell for all of us, but we have each other and that makes a huge difference."

"I can imagine," she said. The empathy in her voice made it seem like things would be even better in the future. He wondered if she'd lost someone important to her.

Zander stopped in front of the Hilton and opened the door to the backseat. Tyler exited first and held out a hand to Jessica. "My lady."

She took the offering with a smile, glancing down at their swamp-filled clothes.

The hotel's manager greeted them at the door. "Mr. O'Brien, what a pleasure to have you back."

It must've taken great effort for her not to wrinkle her nose at the smell of the two of them, Tyler thought. He had to give her credit, she held strong. The manager was tall and brunette, curvy, in her late thirties. Her name tag read Annabeth Malloy.

"Thank you for having us, Miss Malloy," he said, shaking her outstretched hand. "This is my guest Miss Archer."

A bellhop arrived as Annabeth acknowledged Jessica. He'd given a fake name to make Jessica feel more comfortable. She seemed ready to climb out of her skin from the attention they were receiving.

"Devin will help you with your bags," Annabeth said.

"I'm having a few items delivered," Tyler said with a nod toward Devin.

"Of course. Devin will take you to your suite. Please let me know personally if there's anything I can do for you or Miss Archer."

Tyler thanked Annabeth and followed Devin to the elevator, taking Jessica's hand and pulling her close. It was the best way to shield her from any watchful eyes in the hotel lobby. The way she fit with his arm around her felt a little too right. And that was something else Tyler didn't want to think about too much. He had enough going on without further complicating his life. And keeping her alive long enough to find the truth was at the top of his agenda.

"You've been quiet since the car ride," Tyler said, handing Jessica a bag filled with clothes and undergarments, which she eagerly took.

"I feel bad about what I said earlier about your money." She hadn't meant to be a jerk, but she had been. She'd judged him solely based on his money and that made her exactly like the people she despised, the kind of people who only cared about superficial things. The cowboy was nothing like that. He hadn't even hinted at the kind of money he and his brothers had, and she figured he wouldn't have, either. He'd been kind to her and had done nothing but offer help. So what if his presence put her on edge.

"I don't think you're showing it off in any way. In fact, I was a little surprised you had any. No offense."

That deep rumble of a laugh broke free from his chest again and it sent sensual little tingles up and down her body. "I don't know what to say."

She'd showered and was covered head to toe in a thick cotton bathrobe provided by the hotel and yet she was keenly aware of being completely naked underneath.

"It's just that you look so…normal." His skin

was olive colored and tan, and his hands were rough, as if he worked outside.

"What did you expect me to look like?" Thankfully, he seemed amused as he sat down at the expansive oak table in front of a wall of windows that she was sure would frame the best views of the city if the curtains hadn't been pulled shut.

She'd smelled the food the second she'd stepped out of the shower, and despite thinking there was no way she could eat under the circumstances her stomach growled. And he was right, earlier; she did need to keep up her strength.

"Fancy, maybe? Like J.R. Ewing or something," she said, and that solicited a full belly laugh from Tyler.

"Sorry to disappoint you," he said.

"You didn't," she said a little too quickly, and it caused her cheeks to burn. "What I mean to say is that I like that you're normal."

"I could always break out my bolo tie and Western shirts if you'd be more comfortable," he quipped.

"Great. Now you're making fun of me." She reached across the table to slap his arm but he caught her wrist and held it. She didn't immediately move to take it back.

Suddenly the air in the room was charged, and her breath caught in her throat as he drew sexy little circles with his thumb.

Chapter Eight

A tense expression crossed Tyler's features, like he was trying to figure out his next move. He let go of Jessica's wrist and picked up his sandwich instead. "I hope you like BLTs and soup. This won't be as good as Janis's but it'll keep us from starving."

"I'm just happy not to smell like swamp water anymore," she said awkwardly.

"I know you were hoping to find something there and I'm sorry we didn't," he offered.

"Anything would've been nice, some kind of direction." There was so much heat and intensity crackling between them it seemed odd to talk around it.

"Sometimes it's good to be able to rule a place out. My friend Tommy has the motto No Stone Left Unturned during an investigation. It's surprising how a small detail often means the difference between a trail going cold and cracking a case wide-open," he said.

"So, we go back and try to find Elijah's place in Spanish Town," she said.

"Does he know about you?"

"She kept me separate from the rest of her life, even her friends. I doubt she told anyone about me, so he should be quite surprised when her sister shows up on his doorstep."

"Or not."

She cocked her head sideways. "What do you mean?"

"Earlier you suggested trying to fool him into thinking you're Jenn." He paused long enough for her to nod. "She said not to trust anyone. I think we should take her advice to heart. We'll know if he's involved based on his initial reaction to you."

"I hadn't even considered the possibility that one of her friends could've gotten her into this mess, but you're right."

"Let's hope they didn't. But if she's innocent, and I believe you when you say she wouldn't steal, then she either tripped into this or someone set her up," he said. "There aren't a lot of people who would have access to the Infinity Sapphire. We'll track who might've come into contact with the owner over the past few weeks. I'd like to trace your sister's movements as well, but that is a little bit trickier since we don't want to bring you out in the open."

"Speaking of which, I need to do something different with my hair." She rolled a strand around her index finger.

"Supplies were delivered while you were in the shower," he said. "There are hats to choose from. Scarves. We should probably dye your hair and have it cut but your natural color is beautiful."

Butterflies flitted through her stomach at the compliment and she was pretty sure her cheeks flamed. But Jessica wondered if there was anything he couldn't get at the snap of a finger. This was definitely a different lifestyle than the one she knew and it made her more than a little uncomfortable. A man with this kind of money was more Jenn's type. "Thank you."

She finished her sandwich and soup, surprised she was able to clear her plate and bowl. Her body was hungrier than she realized. After changing into linen shorts and a button-down silk blouse, she tried on a couple of hats before settling for one in taupe with a wide brim and a silk scarf wrapped around it. There were tan strappy sandals with just enough of a heel to give her a little more height. She looked in the mirror and hardly recognized herself.

That was most likely a good thing, because even though all of what she wore was out of character for her, she didn't want to look like herself right now.

Jessica applied light makeup, more gifts from the generous millionaire, before walking into the living room where he sat at the desk on his cell phone. Tyler was so down-to-earth that she hadn't thought of him as being wealthy— at least, not until he started flying planes, ordering limousines and generally snapping his fingers to make pretty much anything show up.

None of that should have shocked her, except that he didn't fit the *millionaire* stereotype. Based on her sister's dating stories, rich men sounded like playboys or self-obsessed jerks.

She never could understand what Jenn saw in them. Jenn was beautiful and she could easily turn heads. Even though she and Jessica were identical, Jessica normally looked quite different from her sister. Jessica's hair was pulled up in a ponytail most of the time. She wore very little makeup. And her favorite outfit was a tank top and jeans.

Tyler was different from Jenn's usual men. He was almost staggeringly handsome and definitely good-looking enough to be a playboy, but she was pretty sure he'd laugh if someone said that out loud.

He finished his call and set his cell on the desk in front of him. "The owner of the Infinity Sapphire, Emma-Kate Brasseux, will be home this afternoon."

THE IDEA THAT Tyler could be walking Jessica into the belly of the beast sat in his gut like shards of broken glass. On the other hand, he was darn certain there was no way she was going to let him talk to the owners of the necklace without her. There was far too much at stake. He'd have to be careful not to cross any boundaries with Tommy's investigation and local law enforcement would also be involved. Now that the stolen necklace was common knowledge and the motive in a murder investigation, Tommy would send someone to speak to the Brasseuxs, which was why Tyler wouldn't call ahead and make an appointment to speak with them. He wanted to check things out first.

On the ride over, Tyler wanted to know more about Jessica. "Where's your family, other than your sister?"

"Shreveport, where we grew up. It's just my parents. We had an older brother who died when we were in high school. It affected us both but Jenn hasn't been the same since."

"I'm sorry for your loss." Tyler couldn't imagine losing a sibling so young.

"My brother, Jeffrey, had just turned eighteen and graduated high school when he signed on to work the pipelines in Alaska. Dad had been out of work for a while and my parents were having a hard time keeping food on the table. Sending one of us to college was out of the question.

"Jeffrey noticed an ad in the paper and saw it as his ticket to help the family while getting out on his own. Times were tough and he couldn't find a local job. He hadn't been gone for three months when we heard the news there'd been an accident." Her voice broke, and he could tell that even now it was difficult for her to talk about it.

"Sounds like he was an honorable and brave young man, trying to do the right thing by his family," Tyler said.

Jessica nodded as a tear spilled down her cheek. Tyler thumbed it away. Contact while she was so vulnerable wasn't a good idea. And neither was taking her in his arms, but he did it anyway. He lied and told himself that his actions were purely meant to comfort her. There was so much more to it than that, though... bringing her into his arms calmed his own torn-up heart.

"We were all devastated but Jenn took the news hardest. Something inside her just broke after that. She stopped hanging out with our friends and slept all day for a solid month. When we finally convinced her to get out of bed she was different. She started wearing makeup and spending more time alone. Then she found babysitting jobs and used all the money to buy nicer clothes. In school the next year she started hanging around with rich boys. I think she associated our financial situation with losing Jeffrey. She couldn't get off to college fast enough, relying on school loans to make it happen. It lasted a year before she quit school and moved to Baton Rouge. Said she needed a fresh start. There, she kept her family, including me, under wraps and didn't want us to meet her new friends. I think she was ashamed of us."

Tyler could feel her shaking in his arms, so he hauled her tighter to his chest. The limo had stopped but he didn't care. The only thing that mattered right then was the shaking woman in his arms, the feel of her skin underneath his weathered hands and the way she looked up at him with those big eyes.

So he dipped his head and kissed her. Her body stiffened and then relaxed against him. The shaking stopped as she parted her lips for him and her breath quickened. She brought her hands up around his neck and tunneled her fingers into his hair.

Tyler knew this was charting a dangerous course. He'd cut out casual flings after his first year of college and this woman had already broken through barriers that normally took other women months to breach. He should back off, let go.

He couldn't.

So he deepened the kiss, ignoring all the warning bells trying to sound off inside his head. Jessica dropped her hands, clutching his shirt, and that quieted his internal protest.

Her hand wandered across his chest and he pulled her onto his lap.

The air inside the limo crackled with desperate need.

Desperate.

Tyler didn't like the sound of that word when it came to him and Jessica.

He pulled back and looked into her eyes, a mix of desire and desperation staring back at him.

And that last part was a mood killer.

When they made love—correction, *if* they made love—there'd be nothing desperate about it.

"The car stopped," he said, unable to move…

wishing he'd seen something else in her eyes—
or just good old-fashioned lust.

"I know." She brought the back of her hand
up to her lips and eased off his lap.

Tyler needed a distraction, so he signaled
Zander to lower the partition.

"Where would you go to find someone if
you didn't know their last name or address?"
he asked, focusing on why they were there.
The trip to Spanish Town hadn't taken long.
Other than Elijah's name, they didn't have
much to go on.

"And they live here?" Zander asked.

"Yes."

"Then I'd go to the market. It's a place up
ahead where all the locals gather to eat," Zander said. "I can point you in the direction but
you're not going to find out where someone
lives if you pull up in one of these. It's a tight-
knit community."

"With lots of artists who have an affinity
for pink flamingos, or so I've noticed," Tyler
joked, trying to ease the tension.

Jessica smiled and that helped. He wasn't
sure how he'd allowed things to get so out of
hand in such a short time, but he vowed not to
let it happen again.

"Here's what you want to do." Zander pointed
to the street in front of them. "Go down here

about two blocks. Make a right and walk half-way down the street. The market is dead center of Spanish Town. You can't miss it. If the person you're looking for lives around here, someone will know him or her."

Tyler thanked Zander and asked him to wait right there on the corner. The short walk in the thick humidity, even with cooler overall temperatures, had Tyler plucking at his shirt. Texas was dry in comparison even though his state had seen more rain last year than in any he could remember. He took Jessica's hand in his and she smiled up at him. With that second smile something happened in his chest and he chalked it up to residual feelings from what had happened in the limo. "I think we can get further if people believe we're a couple."

Damned if a hurt look didn't settle in her eyes that knocked the wind out of Tyler. He didn't want to care about Jessica beyond helping to save her and her sister. So what the hell was happening to him? He didn't do mushy feelings but he couldn't ignore the warmth in his chest every time he was near Red. He told himself that it was her situation tugging at his heart. Her brother was gone and her sister's moving away must've hurt like hell. He could never imagine Joshua and Ryder in that situation. But, hey, life was crazy sometimes. And, sometimes, strange things happened.

The market was a grocery-store-turned-eatery where locals gathered for breakfast and lunch. The building was painted fire-engine red and a retractable hunter-green awning covered the sidewalk dining space. The lunch crowd was running thin but Tyler asked for a table for two outside so he could chat up the waitress.

He ordered a shrimp po'boy and two cups of coffee, even though they'd just eaten.

"Will that be all?" the waitress asked. "Dorinda" was stamped on her gold-colored name tag in white letters.

"Yeah, I guess it will. Although, I wonder if you could help me out." Tyler hesitated and she leaned forward. "Our friend Elijah used to play around here. I got a new cell and lost all my contacts." He made an annoyed face that seemed to resonate with Dorinda. "I thought we'd reconnect while we were in town. You know where we can catch him?"

"You just missed him. He was in here a few minutes ago," she said with a small shake of her head.

"Think I can still catch him?" Tyler made a move to get up.

"Stick around long enough and he'll be

back." She motioned toward a waitress inside. "He picks her up as soon as her shift's over."

That was even better news because they didn't know what he looked like. "Do you have any idea what time that will be?"

Dorinda glanced at the white plastic watch on her wrist. "I'd say another hour to an hour and a half."

"Thank you. I can't wait to see that old son of a gun," he said, a little worried he might be overacting.

"Can I get anything else for you, hon?" the waitress asked.

Jessica bent her head forward, face in her hands, as if she had the worst headache of her life. Wearing sunglasses and a wide-brimmed hat, she wouldn't be easily recognized. "Aspirin."

She lifted her head up and laughed. So did Dorinda.

"I told him to stop me after the third Ruby Slipper, but do you think he did?" Jessica said, feigning frustration. She coughed and shook her head.

"I hear you. I'll be right back with those coffees." Dorinda winked before she turned and walked away.

"I hope Elijah comes back soon," Jessica

said, scanning the streets. She had to be un-comfortable out in the open like this.

"I have no intention of allowing anything to happen to you."

Chapter Nine

"We should wait on the corner for Elijah," Tyler said. "We don't know what he looks like but we know who he's coming to pick up. This way no one will get suspicious if he walks right past us."

Jessica agreed as she followed him. He stopped and turned toward her, shielding her from the street.

"Are you doing okay?" he asked, and then brushed the tips of his fingers against her cheek in a move that sent sensual shivers skittering across her skin.

Her back was against the telephone pole at N. Seventh Street and Spanish Town Road, directly across the street from where they'd eaten. Cars twined down the skinny road.

Jessica nodded as she studied the activity. "This guy walked by a few minutes ago."

"Which one?" Tyler's gaze swept the sidewalk casually.

"This guy in the white pants, white hat." She intentionally looked in the opposite direction.

"He seems to be interested in us," he said, and he couldn't ignore the possibility that the police or others—men with guns—wanted to find the same person they were looking for.

The next thing Jessica knew, Tyler's hand had cupped her neck. He mouthed the words, *Trust me.* And then he dipped his head, hesitated, slicked his tongue across his lips and kissed her.

Her body instantly reacted. She reached for him, wrapping her arms around his neck and parting her mouth enough for his tongue to slide inside.

She thought she heard a groan from deep in his throat as his arm came around her waist and his free hand splayed against her back.

Deepening the kiss, he hugged her—her body immediately molding to his. Her breasts swelled and ached for his touch. Her body reminded her just how long it had been since she'd had good sex…and it had been far too long. She instinctively sensed that sex with Tyler would shatter her in the best possible way.

His body pressed hers against the telephone

pole and she imagined how he would feel on top of her, pressing her into a mattress. She could feel his rapid heartbeat through their clothes.

He pulled back first and rested his forehead on hers. From across the street someone shouted, "Get a room!"

The comment made both of them laugh, his was that low rumble from deep in his throat and it was so darn sexy. He started to say something, then stopped, and she half feared that he was about to offer an apology. That was the best kiss she'd had in…in her whole life, and a part of her wanted to celebrate it, not feel awkward that it had happened.

"Damn," he said and his voice was low.

"I was just thinking the same thing," she said with a slow smile. His hand stayed steady against her back and she was grateful because he was the only thing holding her upright at this point. Her bones felt like Jell-O. She'd heard that a kiss could make a person go weak at the knees but this was the first time she'd experienced anything close.

"I've been wanting to do that again since we stepped out of the limo," he whispered.

"Maybe you should try it one more time." She tunneled her fingers into his dark curly hair.

He didn't seem to need much encouragement

because he delved his tongue inside her mouth with bruising need. His body pressed against hers, sandwiching her, and desire sprang from deep within. In that moment, she got lost.

Tyler seemed to regain his senses first, pulling back. All the warmth in the cowboy's eyes turned to something else…something that looked a lot like confusion, and it caused her heart to squeeze.

"We should be watching out for Elijah. He could be here by now."

"Did I do something wrong?" she asked.

"You? Hell, no. But I just crossed a line that I shouldn't have, and I apologize," he said.

Where had that come from? And to make matters worse, he just apologized for kissing her.

Embarrassed, she sidestepped him. "Don't be sorry. I participated just as much as you did."

"Come over here. I'll kiss you, honey" came from a few steps away with inappropriate smooching noises.

If that didn't set her cheeks on fire, then waiting wordlessly with the cowboy standing next to her did. Sure he regretted their actions after having a chance to think about it. Jessica didn't doubt she was attractive, especially when she put on nice clothes and some makeup, but this wealthy cowboy was out of her league and he had to know as much as she did that it would never work between them. It would be smart to keep her guard up with him. As soon as she found her sister and settled this mess, she'd go back to her life in Shreveport, a life that made total sense.

The waitress, Elijah's presumed girlfriend, came out the front door, lit a smoke and leaned against the front glass of the restaurant. Someone knocked on the window from inside. She made a face and moved over to the newspaper boxes at the side of the red building.

A full twenty minutes later a vintage El Camino pulled up. It had been partially restored, looked like a work in progress and had the beginnings of a mural painted down the right hand side.

The waitress pushed off the wall of the market. Now on her second smoke, she looked at the driver of the El Camino. She hesitated, made another face and then started walking toward the curb.

Jessica pulled off her hat and glasses and rushed toward the El Camino. "Elijah."

The man driving was in his early thirties and fit the description of a Louisiana musician to a T. He wore a chestnut fedora with a white hatband and red feather. Both arms were covered in tattoos and he wore a dark tank underneath a denim shirt with rolled-up sleeves. He had a silver thumb ring on his left hand, dark hair and eyes, and a mustache and goatee.

"Jenn, where the hell have you been?" he asked, eyes bright.

A moment of panic engulfed Jessica. Could she pull off being her sister when so much was on the line? Sure, it had been easy enough when she was stepping in to ease Jenn out of a relationship. But this? This was so much more nerve racking.

Jessica smiled as she pulled Tyler over to the El Camino's passenger side so Elijah could get a good look. She came up with the best lie she could. "I met someone and we ended up at his place in New Orleans."

Elijah shook his head and smirked. "I should've known. You could at least answer my texts."

"Lost my charger." She shrugged, figuring that was exactly something that would've happened to her less responsible sister.

"Actually, she lost her phone altogether," Tyler said, sticking his hand out. "I'm George For... Ford."

Jessica, arm around his waist, pinched him. Seriously? That slip might've just cost them. It would be a miracle if Elijah bought that...

"Good to meet you," Elijah said, no hint of distrust at Tyler's hesitation.

Even so, Tyler didn't seem to be good at this undercover thing. Or maybe lying didn't come naturally to him. That was a good thing considering her ex, Brent, had seemed to wake up with lies coming out of his mouth. Lies like *you're the one I love* and *what we have is real* were right up there with *she didn't mean anything to me.* Her name had been Katherine. And Jessica had believed him the first time. Then she'd stumbled across his secret email account and had been forced to ask him if Katherine had been the one he was talking about, or was it Naomi, Judy or Blanche?

Thankfully, Elijah didn't seem to notice Tyler's mistake.

"I see you've moved on from one millionaire to another," Elijah said with a wink.

Was she supposed to know what that meant?

The waitress pushed past them and plopped into the passenger seat, looking annoyed that she hadn't been acknowledged yet.

"My friend, Susannah." He looked from the waitress to Jessica.

"Girlfriend," Susannah interjected with an annoyed slap to his right forearm.

"Nice to meet you," Jessica said, appreciating the distraction. If Elijah didn't look too closely or ask too many questions then she could keep up the charade.

"Well, George, the next time you whisk my girl out of town without telling anyone make sure she checks in with me, okay? Big Beau's been looking for you, by the way." He made a face at Jessica.

The reference drew another blank.

Then again, Jenn had been secretive lately. She'd said she was dating someone important but didn't say who.

Tyler glanced from Elijah to her. He slid his arm around her waist—she ignored the quiver that rippled through her stomach—and squeezed her so her side was flush with his. He repositioned her in front of him and wrapped his arms around her.

"Do I need to be worried about Big Beau?" he asked against her neck loud enough for Elijah to hear, his breath heating her skin.

She shook her head and her cheeks heated. Thankfully, her blush was authentic. Her body was a pinball machine of electrical impulses with Tyler this close. At least she didn't have to fake an attraction. Jessica might have the ability to sell a lie, she'd done it for her sister, but that didn't mean she enjoyed doing it.

Elijah looked at her and it seemed like he was

really examining her. That wasn't good. "Are we good for Thanksgiving, then? My place?"

"Of course," she said raising her voice a few octaves like Jenn did when she was flirting. She twined a strand of hair around her finger and smiled, using all her sister's charms against him.

"You're not going to ditch me for him, right?" he asked, pain from the past still present in his eyes. She felt bad for him because she knew exactly what it was like when Jenn decided to make other plans. It was warm in the sunlight and cold in the shadows.

"Why would I do that?" she frowned. Exaggerating the expression was exactly Jenn's style and made Jessica want to throw up in her mouth a little bit. Her sister had a flare for drama.

Elijah shot her a glare. "Now, that's a good question. Why would you stand me up when we have plans?"

Jessica loved her sister and she'd never want her hurt, but she could get easily frustrated with Jenn's personality and the way she treated people at times. Elijah stared at Jessica and she realized that she'd missed an inside reference between Elijah and Jenn. She'd missed a cue and now Elijah was suspicious. Frustration nipped at her. It was difficult to think straight with her back pressed against Tyler's pure muscle-over-steel chest.

This situation was getting sticky.

"I hate to take her away from you, but we have reservations," Tyler said, catching on.

Elijah had already looked her up and down as though suddenly realizing this was not an outfit Jenn would ever have on her body. Panic was beginning to set in. The exchange wasn't a total loss. They'd gotten the name Big Beau from him but who the heck was that?

The waitress in the passenger seat was looking a little annoyed. "Good. Maybe we can go now?"

There was a hint of jealousy in her tone. Did Elijah have real feelings for Jenn? Maybe that was the weird vibe she was picking up on from him.

"Stop by later," he said, ignoring Susannah, who looked even less thrilled now.

Tyler tugged at Jessica's hip. She almost forgot to blow a kiss to Elijah and that was something her sister always did before she walked away. Jessica turned and thanked heaven she had, because Elijah was staring expectantly. She blew the kiss and he smiled widely before pulling away.

"He almost caught me," she said to Tyler as they doubled back to walk to where the limo had parked. "My sister always blows a kiss. It's the silliest thing and I nearly forgot to do it."

Tyler squeezed her, keeping his arm around her as they walked. "You did good. He seemed suspicious at first when you missed that personal reference, but then he relaxed."

"I really thought I blew it," she said honestly. "Thank you for saving me."

"No problem. And now we have a name," he said with more than a hint of pride in his tone.

"Think we can go back to the market and ask around?" she asked.

"It's not safe for us here," he said. The weight of those words was heavy on her limbs. He was right. They'd dodged one bullet with Elijah and they needed to get out of Spanish Town.

"Big Beau. That could be anybody," she said under her breath.

"We'll have to ask around, but my guess is that someone will know who he is."

The limo was parked exactly where they'd left it. Zander stepped out as soon as he saw them and then opened the back door.

"Where to, Mister Tyler?" Zander asked.

"18008 North Mission Hills Avenue," Tyler said, conceding the *mister*.

"I'm probably just being paranoid, but do

you get the feeling that someone's been following us?" Jessica asked.

"Yes, and I haven't decided if that's a good or bad thing yet."

18008 NORTH MISSION HILLS Avenue was one of those luxurious, one-of-a-kind New Orleans–style estates. Tyler had said the Brasseuxs lived there. The grounds looked like a park and it reminded Jessica of the grand homes of the old South. The place had been meticulously constructed with old brick, a slate roof and patios, and an oversize front porch with columns and one of those Southern-style front entrances. It was exactly the image that came to mind when Jessica thought of old Baton Rouge money. A golf course wound through the neighborhood and she guessed there had to be at least four or five acres of lush, flawlessly groomed grounds around this house alone.

Zander pulled up to the front gate and idled the engine. The partition slid down. "This the place where you're headed, Mister Tyler?"

"Doesn't look like we'll get past the gate without an appointment," Tyler said.

"No, it doesn't. What would you like to do?"

Tyler's hand was already on the door release. "I believe we'll get out here. Why don't you circle around the neighborhood? I'll call you as soon as we're ready to be picked up."

"Yes, sir," Zander said.

Jessica followed Tyler into the unseasonably sticky air, missing the air-conditioning as soon as she stepped out of the limo.

"I hope we make it to the main house. Security could be all over us long before we make it halfway across the yard," he said.

Surprisingly, they did make it. Majestic live oaks surrounded the house. As they neared, she saw something that made her heart jump in her chest—the partially painted El Camino parked at the side.

Jessica froze. "Elijah's here?"

Tyler shot her a look that warned her to be on guard. "We have no idea if we're here because we outsmarted security or if we're right where they want us. Either way, I'd like to get a closer look."

"He must be involved," she said quietly and mostly to herself. There must've been something she'd missed in their conversation. He hadn't missed a beat when he saw her. But then, she wasn't the best judge when it came to liars. Jessica had the sometimes unfortunate tendency to take people at face value. "Do you think this means my sister is somewhere safe?"

"It very well might." There was a note of

sympathy in his voice. He was trying to give her hope and she appreciated it. She would hold on to it and not give in to the despair nipping at her heels.

The veranda stretched on for what felt like days, wrapping the entire front and left side of the mansion. There were half a dozen white rockers positioned to take advantage of the view of the front gardens. She followed Tyler to a window and peeked inside. She'd already seen the hand-painted stained-glass windows from the front yard. But what they could see through the window was the picture of opulence.

The crystal chandelier hanging over the foyer was fit for a king. Jessica moved to the next set of windows to the left and saw a receiving room that looked like something out of a Southern plantation magazine. A marble fireplace mantel was the focal point of the room. There were perfectly preserved vintage gold-leafed French furnishings. This place was the very epitome of grandeur—a world that was very foreign to Jessica. Even though it was beautiful, it was also intimidating and felt like something out of another time and place, albeit perfectly preserved.

"Whoever decorated this place must've died in the Civil War," Tyler joked, and she was once again reminded of how different he was from the picture of wealthy people that Jenn had painted.

She couldn't help but laugh and it felt good to break the tension. "I can't see Elijah anywhere."

"I don't like that one bit," Tyler admitted.

Jessica's stomach dropped when she heard the sound of a boot stepping onto the wooden porch. She whirled and there he was, fifteen feet away, the barrel of a gun pointed at her.

"Don't even think about doing anything stupid, cowboy," Elijah said as Tyler spun around.

"Funny seeing you here," Tyler quipped, holding his hands up in surrender. "I'm here to see the Brasseuxs. Emma-Kate's expecting us."

"She and Ashton aren't here right now," Elijah said with an ominous smirk.

Jessica thought when she'd first seen Elijah's El Camino that he was somehow in league with the Brasseuxs. Now she wondered if that had been a mistake. Maybe he was just a common criminal and they were innocent victims. "Where is she?"

"Who?"

"Don't play dumb. You know exactly who I'm talking about," Jessica said.

"Jenn? Let's just say she won't be in the way anymore." His voice held no emotion.

Jessica cursed and made a move toward Elijah, blinded by anger.

Tyler stopped her by grabbing her arm. "Don't. That's exactly what he wants. Don't give him any reason to shoot you."

She conceded but took another step forward, hoping she could get Tyler close enough to make a move. Elijah couldn't shoot both of them and she might be able to create a diversion long enough to give Tyler an advantage. She knew nothing about guns, though, so she had no idea if Elijah could fire multiple rounds in a few seconds or if he'd need to cock the hammer every time. Tyler squeezed her elbow and she took that as a warning.

"What do you want with me?" she asked, still trying to stall so Tyler could think of a plan. She knew he wouldn't make a move as long as that barrel was pointed at her chest. She didn't need to be an expert to know that a shot this close would do serious damage.

"Who the hell are you? Jenn never said anything about having a sister," Elijah said and his voice was a study in calm. His disposition, relaxed shoulders and steady hand said that he felt in control, and he was for the moment.

"It's none of your business who I am," she

shot back, anger getting the best of her again. The gentle, reassuring squeeze to her arm came a second later. "Where is my sister?"

Elijah sighed. "That, I don't know."

"You're lying." Jessica ground her back teeth to keep from saying anything else that might provoke him. She saw a figure moving toward them using the live oaks as cover out of her peripheral vision. Zander?

"Now that you're here, I have to figure out what to do with you both," Elijah said.

She needed to distract him so Zander could get closer. "My sister trusted you. She thought you were a friend. Why would you do this to her?"

His laugh was almost a cackle. "Your sister looks out for number one. Just like I do. She, of all people, would understand me putting myself first."

"She wouldn't hurt a flea and you know it."

"Tell that to Mrs. Brasseux," he quipped. "After all, Jenn was sleeping with her husband."

Was her sister having an affair with a married man? Was that the reason she'd kept her new man's identity a secret?

"Take me to her. Please," Jessica begged, trying to process that last bit of information.

"He can't," Tyler finally spoke up. "He isn't the one calling the shots."

"That's not your concern. And that goes for both of you," Elijah shot back defensively. His lips thinned. His gaze narrowed. Tyler clearly had struck a nerve.

"Then tell me who is," Jessica said. Her sister had always spoken highly of Elijah. "If you cared about my sister at all you wouldn't do this."

"Move." Elijah motioned toward the porch steps.

Tyler urged her forward, moving his hand low on her back.

"Hands up where I can see them," Elijah said.

"Where are the Brasseuxs?" Tyler asked.

"Let's just say they're preoccupied at the moment. Now move." Elijah gestured with the barrel of his gun. He was taking them to his El Camino. There was no trunk, thankfully, because Jessica was claustrophobic and she feared she'd have a panic attack.

As they rounded the corner of the big house, she noticed there was another car parked in front of the El Camino, a white sedan. The El Camino had been blocking the second car from view. Jessica heard a click and the trunk automatically opened.

Jessica's chest squeezed and the heavy air thinned as she thought about climbing into that trunk. No way would her claustrophobia allow her to go inside there willingly. Her body began to shake. If she could keep her cool, Elijah might take her right to Jenn. Then again, he could just take them into the bayou, shoot them and dump their bodies into the swamp for the alligators to pick apart.

More than anything she wanted to glance backward to see if Zander was making progress toward them but she couldn't risk giving him away.

Elijah made Jessica and Tyler walk in front of him, and he was giving them a wide enough berth to make it impossible for Tyler to disarm him. He sure thought like a criminal for someone who'd been parading around as a musician. If what Elijah had said was true and he had no idea where Jenn was, then Jessica and Tyler were in big trouble.

A struggle sounded behind them and a bullet split the air. Jessica instinctively ducked, but before she could get her bearings someone was on top of her and she was facedown on the concrete parking pad with a masculine body shielding her. Tyler's body. And he had a calming presence.

"Stay low," was all she heard him say before

another shot fired. "Get behind the house as fast as you can. Don't look back."

Panic nearly closed her throat as the pressure of his body eased and she scrambled for cover. She couldn't help but look back to see if Tyler or Zander had been shot. All she could see clearly was Tyler diving into the fray. There was blood on the concrete and her heart stuttered as she rounded the corner, looking for something she could use to help the guys. No way would she leave them alone to deal with Elijah if there was something she could do to help.

There was nothing around so she ran to the back porch and tried the door. Locked. Dammit.

Another shot was fired and she ran to the corner of the building to see what had happened. Before she could get a good visual, Tyler was helping Zander toward her as the El Camino sped off. Blood dripped from the arm dangling at Zander's side and she rushed to help him. "What happened?"

Zander winced as he moved. "Bullet grazed my shoulder. I'll be fine. I saw you two in trouble and had to help—the police wouldn't have come in time."

"We appreciate it." Tyler helped Zander to the rear porch. "Where's your cell?"

"Back pocket." Zander eased to one side as Tyler fished out the phone.

"I'm calling for an ambulance. We'll stick around until they get close and then we have to go. Her sister's in danger and we can't afford to lose any more time," Tyler said as he pulled off his undershirt and tied it around Zander's shoulder just above the wound while checking to make sure Elijah wasn't circling back. "You're going to be fine. Have the police check on the family inside the house, if anyone's there."

Zander nodded. "Don't worry about me. Nothing but a scratch."

Wasn't that pretty much the same line all men gave? If the situation weren't so dire, Jessica would laugh.

"Keys fell out of my pocket. Heard them drop over there somewhere." Zander motioned toward a pool of blood. "Take the limo and get out of here."

Tyler handed the cell to Zander, who explained that he'd had an altercation and needed help.

Jessica located the fanned-out keys. "Got 'em."

"Then go," Zander pressed after ending the call.

"Not until help arrives," Tyler said.

"I'll tell the cops that I ran into someone in town who asked me to drop him off here. I'll give them the description of the man who drew a gun on you and Jessica. That way the police will be looking for him and not either of you." Zander took his cell phone and wiped it down. "Can't have your prints on here."

"What will you tell them about your limo disappearing?" Tyler asked, thanking Zander.

"I'll figure something out. Don't worry." Zander shooed them away as sirens sounded far in the distance. "I'm fine. Now go."

"We'll check on you later," Tyler said, embracing Zander in a man-hug. "Thank you for everything you've done. We wouldn't be alive without you."

Jessica's sister, on the other hand, might not have been so lucky.

Chapter Ten

"Do you think it's possible what Elijah said is true?" Jessica asked. The Louisiana humidity made it difficult to breathe.

"That your sister was having an affair with Ashton?" Tyler navigated the limo onto the highway.

"She had a new man in her life and she refused to tell me who he was," she said, tapping on the dashboard.

"Makes for a good story. Your sister is having an affair with a wealthy man. Tries to get him to leave his wife but he won't. She steals his wife's family heirloom for revenge," he said.

"When you put it like that, it sounds like something on a TV crime show."

"Exactly. And it sums everything up nicely except the part where your sister's not a thief," he said, and then glanced over at her. "You haven't changed your mind, have you?"

She hesitated. "Not really. I know my sister. But then I wouldn't have believed that she was involved with a married man, and yet she is."

"True." There was no conviction in his voice. "She may not have known he was married when she met him."

Good point. For all her social climbing, she was still a small-town girl at heart. A sophisticated liar could pull the wool over Jenn's eyes.

"Also, in the last message she said not to believe what Milton would say about her. Maybe the same holds true for Elijah. I think we need to talk to your sister before we jump to any conclusions," he said.

"What do you think the name Big Beau really means?" Jessica asked.

"He could've been throwing the name out to get a reaction from you," Tyler said.

"A reaction from my sister," she clarified. "Or so he thought at the time."

"My bet is that Big Beau is an actual person," Tyler said. "We'll start there. The only other clue we have is the bayou."

"I still don't know if that's significant." She couldn't help the desperation in her voice.

"Milton's still out there somewhere, most likely looking for you," he said. "It would help if we knew what your sister had been doing and where she'd been leading up to this. Does Jenn keep a diary or journal?"

"No. She's not really the type to actually write anything down. Her cell phone is a different story. If we could find that then we'd get more of the picture of what's going on. She and her cell are inseparable." Jessica pinched the bridge of her nose to stave off a headache. "Where to next?"

"We need to find a good place to hide this limo and get back to our hotel to clean up and figure out our next move." Tyler pulled a business card out of his pocket. He handed the card and his cell to Jessica, temporarily steering with his left hand.

Annabeth Malloy, the hotel manager?

"Call her number and put the phone on speaker," he instructed.

A few seconds later the familiar voice was on the line.

"This is Tyler O'Brien—"

"Of course, Mr. O'Brien, how can I help you?"

"I'd like to enter through the service door. A society reporter's been bothering my friend and I and we'd like to shake him."

"No problem at all, sir," she said. "I'll make

the arrangements and have someone waiting for you."

"Excellent. Much appreciated," he said. "There's one more thing, I'd like my limo safely stored until I need it again."

"Absolutely," she said confidently.

"Much obliged, ma'am."

Jessica got lost in her thoughts for the rest of the drive, rolling over the new information about her sister.

The service entrance was dead quiet and empty, not a soul in sight. The sticky humidity made Jessica want to shower all over again. Adrenaline had faded. She was tired and hungry. At least the air-conditioning in their suite evened out her temperature.

"I need to clean up." She disappeared into the bathroom, not wanting the cowboy to see the tears brimming in her eyes. The past day and a half had been surreal and a very real fear engulfed her every time she thought about her sister. Some people believed in twin telepathy and there were moments when Jessica did, too. Instances like this one, when she was overwhelmed with fear for her sister and she was sure something bad was happening.

"If we put our heads together, we'll figure out where your sister is," Tyler reassured her as she stepped out of the bathroom in fresh clothes. This time, she'd opted for a simple T-shirt and cotton shorts with running shoes. Her hair was thrown up in a ponytail; it kept her neck cooler that way.

She nodded but didn't say anything. What could she say? Her sister had never felt farther away.

"You could get away with calling yourself a college student dressed like that," Tyler said in an obvious attempt to change the subject. He seemed to pick up on her mood. "LSU isn't far and that look should help you blend in."

"Thank you. I think."

"It was meant as a compliment. Order whatever you want from room service. Would you mind asking them to send up a burger and a beer for me?"

"Not at all." In fact, both sounded really good right now.

"Thanks. I'll just be in there taking a cold shower." He seemed to realize the implication in that last part and he cracked a dry smile. "For that reason, too, but I need to wash the blood off me."

Jessica couldn't help but smile. For a wealthy guy, he was the most down-to-earth man she'd met. The images of the type of men her sister had dated paraded around in her head. She imagined flashy suits and designer casual wear. This cowboy was pretty much the polar opposite. And he looked damn good in his jeans and boots, so much better than those superficial types.

Normally, she'd notice more about the handsome cowboy, but all she could really focus on right now was Jenn. Besides, her thoughts were only more confused about Tyler after the couple of kisses they'd shared.

Jessica absently dialed room service and ordered dinner. The sun was going down and they still had no answers. Questions swirled. All they knew for sure was that her sister was in trouble, so nothing new there.

Tyler joined her fifteen minutes later, wearing only a pair of jeans that sat low on his hips. His rippled chest was tanned and muscled. Working on a ranch sure as heck did a body good because he had a six pack below solid steel pecs.

"Food should be here soon," she said, trying to force her eyes away from his chest. "And I'm not any closer to figuring out where my sister could be than I was this morning."

The couch dipped under Tyler's weight as he sat down next to her. She'd pulled a notepad and pen from on top of the nightstand and made a few scribbles on it. Mostly, the word *bayou* sat in the middle of the page and she'd circled it over and over again until it looked like one thick mass of wires.

"We just need one break. That's all. And we'll figure this whole thing out. What else do you remember about coming here with her?" the handsome cowboy asked, and no matter how many hours she spent with him she'd never get used to the sound of his voice. Its deep timbre stirred her somewhere low in her belly, and the flutter of a thousand butterflies rippled through her every time he spoke.

"She used to order in a lot when I visited. I didn't really think about it much before but I guess she didn't want to be seen with me." She wrote down the words *Big Beau*. "Do you think Elijah was just trying to throw us off?"

Tyler shrugged as the phone rang. They both looked at the land line.

"Could be the front desk," Jessica offered.

Tyler answered. "It's Zander. He's calling from a phone at the ER."

She heard very little from Tyler's end, which meant that Zander was doing all the talking. The instant Tyler hung up, she asked, "Is he okay?"

"He's doing fine. Said one of the bullets tapped his shoulder and the other grazed the inside of his arm and his ribs, missing anything that could cause serious damage. The doctor said he's very lucky." Tyler walked over to the couch and she couldn't help but admire his athletic grace. Basic biology had her evaluating whether or not he could protect her, given that they were in such dangerous circumstances. "They're treating and releasing him."

"That's the best news I've heard all day." She sighed with relief.

A knock sounded at the door. Tyler shot her a warning look. "Get out of sight until I give you a green light."

She moved into the bedroom and stood behind the door where she could see through the crack.

Tyler pulled a handgun, she wasn't sure what kind, and held it behind his leg as he opened the door with his left hand.

"Come on in," he said to the room service attendant.

The attendant wore a white sous chef shirt and black pants. He looked legit as he wheeled in the tray. "Would you like me to set up at the table, Mr. O'Brien?"

"No, thanks. Just leave it there." Tyler pointed next to the table. "I can take it from here."

He pulled a few bills from his pocket and tipped the attendant without revealing what was in his other hand. "Smells fantastic."

"Enjoy, sir," the waiter said with a smile.

Tyler closed the door behind him. "It's safe."

Even though the waiter was gone and the coast was clear, the tension stayed in the room. Jessica hated living like this, afraid of her own shadow. But her identity had been revealed and soon everyone would know that Jenn had a twin sister.

"What are you thinking about?" Tyler placed the gun securely in the side table.

"How they're not going to stop until they find me. They know about me now. Our advantage is gone."

He motioned for her to sit at the table, so she did. He put a plate in front of her and pulled off the metal cover to reveal the best-looking hamburger she'd ever seen. Or maybe she was just that hungry.

"I also ordered a fresh pot of coffee," she said. After that adrenaline rush, the beer didn't sound as good as coffee. She didn't want anything to dull her senses and she was a lightweight when it came to alcohol.

He must've been thinking the same thing because he set the beers aside in an ice bucket. "I'll keep these cold for later."

By the time she took the last bite of her burger, Jessica had downed a bottled water. She poured a cup of coffee afterward. "Want one?"

"I can get it."

"I'm right here." She cocked her eyebrow. She hadn't noticed it with all the drama going on around them, but this cowboy seemed to prefer to do everything for himself. "I don't mind. Really."

"Don't go to any trouble."

"It's none at all." She poured a cup and handed it to him. "See how easy that was?"

He chuckled. "My parents taught us to be independent. We grew up working the ranch right alongside Pop. Mom spoiled us but pretended not to. She always said we were blessed and not spoiled. Either way she managed to bring up six independent boys. Although," he smiled, "some might call us stubborn."

"Sounds like you grew up in an ideal family."

"We did. And it ruined us. We all have a difficult time letting others in," he admitted and there was something dark in his eyes now. Regret?

"Doesn't sound like such a bad thing. The situation I'm in now reminds me to be even more careful who I trust," she said. "Even someone with the best of intentions can hurt you."

"Trust can be a good thing. When it's earned." Had he trusted Lyndsey too soon? He'd believed that she knew him and understood his priorities. And then she'd demanded that he walk away from the ranch forever if he wanted a future with her. She'd said their life was in Denver, where her family lived. Needless to say, being given an ultimatum had gone over about as well as filthy ranch clothes in church and begged the question, why would she demand something like that if she really knew him?

She'd walked out and the nagging question remained: How could he have loved someone he knew so little? Even so, when Lyndsey had left he didn't think he'd ever breathe again. Surprisingly, his body functioned even when he wasn't sure he wanted it to. Losing his parents at the same time had been a double blow.

Speaking of family, when this ordeal was over and Jessica was safe, he needed to touch base with his brothers and Tommy about the investigation back home. It was easy to set aside his pain and focus on someone else's problem for a change. Tyler had focused on his own until he'd gone numb. All he could think about was the note Lyndsey had left behind. *Enjoy your life and try to put someone else first for a change.*

For the past few weeks he'd tried to figure

out if there was any truth to what she'd said. He'd dated around since Lyndsey, but it had felt like he was ticking a box, making sure he was playing the field.

Tyler could be honest enough with himself to admit that Lyndsey hadn't been completely first in his life. He chalked it up to their differences. She was outgoing and liked to hang out with friends at the bar after a long day. She was flirtatious and he'd almost convinced himself that he didn't mind. He was the complete opposite. Tyler kept more to himself, preferring to trust only those who shared the O'Brien last name.

And after a long day, he wanted a good meal and a cold beer under the stars. If there was a woman involved, then he could think of other things he wanted to do, as well…things that involved both of them naked.

There was something special about looking up at the night sky in Texas, the wide expanse of midnight blue with bright specks.

Lyndsey was most likely right. He probably needed to make more of an effort with people. He was good at negotiating and analyzing all sides of a business deal to come up with a fair solution and that's why he was in charge of handling contracts and disputes. He had managed a temporary truce between Aunt Bea and Uncle Ezra recently and that had taken some serious skills. But dealing with emotions, especially his own, wasn't his strong suit.

Enough focus on the things he didn't have the first idea how to fix.

Tyler needed to straighten out his thoughts about the current situation. "Let's go back to the beginning and think this through. Milton was one of your sister's exes, right?"

"Yes. She dated him for a short while last year but they stayed friends after, or so she thought." Jessica sat on the couch and folded her right leg underneath her bottom. She sipped her coffee and set the mug on the table.

"Is that the reason she figured he wouldn't catch on that you were subbing for her? He must not've known her very well," Tyler said.

"He didn't. Not really. But then my sister's personality has many layers. I'm not sure I know all of her. I never imagined she'd be in any kind of trouble like this and yet here we are. And then there's the affair."

"We now know that Elijah is involved," he said.

"Up to his eye teeth," she added.

"How close were the two of them?"

"I'm guessing he reminded her of home,

barely scraping by," she said. "He must've felt familiar to her and helped her miss us less."

"I can't help but wonder how a musician and a corporate lawyer would know each other. It doesn't seem that they would travel in the same circles," he said. "Not to mention the fact that Milton couldn't possibly be currently practicing law with his criminal record."

"That's a good question. My sister is the only connection I can find. She never dated Elijah to my knowledge." Jessica sipped her coffee.

"But that doesn't mean he didn't have feelings for her."

"No. You're right. In fact, I'm pretty sure he did based on the way he looked at me before. There was no way she'd go out with him, though," Jessica's eyes lit up just then. Her eyes weren't the only thing he noticed. There were other things, endearing quirks about her that he liked. For example, the corner of her mouth twitched when she was nervous. The movement was so slight he almost missed it the first time. He'd also noticed that her tongue slicked across her bottom lip when she was about to lie. He'd seen that a few times when she spoke to Elijah and was grateful that she hadn't done it while talking to him.

Her laugh was almost like music and made him want to hear it more often. He vowed to himself to take her out to dinner when this was all behind them and make her laugh until her stomach hurt. Also, she blinked when she wasn't sure what to say next.

But the main thing he noticed was how sweet she tasted when he kissed her. And just how right she fit when he'd held her in his arms.

"I'm worried about the Brasseuxs." She sighed sharply. "And I feel like a hamster on a wheel. Every time I ask questions I go round again."

"I keep wondering what they and Elijah have in common. Or Milton, for that matter." Tyler stabbed his fingers through his thick hair. "I mean, the Brasseuxs could've had some interaction with Milton socially. But Elijah? I can't find a connection there."

"I know one," Jessica said.

Tyler arched a brow.

"My sister," Jessica said quietly. "What if she's not as innocent as I want to believe? What if she stole the necklace to get back at Ashton and then her so-called friend Elijah sees an opportunity to make some money off of her?

Everything could've gone sour and she got herself in more trouble than she could handle."

"You don't really believe that, do you?" he asked.

"I don't want to, but that's where the evidence points," she said. "You know what? I'm tired. I need to get some rest."

Chapter Eleven

Jessica tossed and turned in her bed, unable to sleep for the nagging feeling that she was missing something important. She drifted in and out, straining to think. At three o'clock in the morning it finally dawned on her. She bolted upright and must've screamed because Tyler burst into the room a few seconds later.

"What happened?" he said, his low, sexy voice still gravelly from sleep. He rubbed his eyes and moved to the bed.

"I didn't mean to wake you," she said, forcing her eyes away from his muscled chest. This wasn't the time to think about those ripples of pure steel and how soft his skin felt to her touch. Or the warmth his body possessed.

"I'm a light sleeper." The mattress dipped under his weight. He had on boxers and nothing else.

"It came to me in a flash and I realized what

I'd been missing. Do you have your smartphone?" she asked.

He jogged into the next room, returned a moment later and offered his cell to her.

She pulled up the internet and entered *The Bayou* into the search engine. Hope filled her chest for the first time. "It's an actual place. The Bayou. She said that she'd see me in the bayou, which I assumed was a general reference, except that there really is a place. She took me there the very first time I visited and never again. It was one of the only public places we went. It's really far on the outskirts of town. Actually, saying it's near any kind of civilization is being generous."

"What kind of place is it?" he asked.

"A hole-in-the-wall that only locals know about. See?" She shoved the phone toward him with an address highlighted on Google Maps. "It doesn't have a website, per se, but it's listed as a business. This is the address."

He took the phone and examined the web page. "This is a good place to start."

In her excitement at this first real lead, she launched herself toward Tyler and threw her arms around his neck. The covers pooled around her knees.

"This place looks…interesting to say the

least. It's literally surrounded by a swamp." His free arm circled her waist.

Jessica realized all too quickly that her thin cotton tank top was the only thing standing between them. She started to pull back.

He dropped the phone on the bed next to her knees.

"Oh, no you don't," he said, hauling her against his chest. His other arm wrapped around her bottom.

Before she could talk herself out of it, she kissed him. With a quick maneuver, he had her on his lap, straddling him, and she could feel the warmth of his erection pulsing against the inside of her thigh. Jessica deepened the kiss. Tyler was all hotness and fire and manliness. His hands palmed her bottom. She liked the feel of him…real…and rough…and still so surprisingly gentle. She scooted closer until her heat was positioned against his straining rod. The thought of sex with Tyler sent a thunderclap of need pounding through her, making her stomach quiver.

His hands roamed her bottom as she pressed her almost-naked breasts flush against his chest.

A throaty, sexy growl tore from his throat and she could feel his muscles as they flexed. Their breath quickened as her hands searched down his back, lingering on each ripple, memorizing his strong lines.

And then five words she didn't want to acknowledge wound through her thoughts. *Is this a good idea?*

She barely knew the guy and yet she'd already trusted him with her life. And a certain intimacy had come out of that, which couldn't be denied. But did she really know him? Sure, the sexual tension between them was thicker than the Louisiana humidity. She had no doubt sex with Tyler would be amazing. And then what?

They were from two different worlds. He'd go back to his life on the ranch. She'd go back to hers in Shreveport, helping her parents and running the family business, which wasn't much but enough to keep them going financially. She couldn't imagine leaving them to fend for themselves.

Her brain cautioned her not to get ahead of herself. The future was a long way away. She had tonight. She was feeling the effects of an exciting breakthrough. And there was nothing wrong with mindless sex.

THE IDEA OF taking a breather when Jessica's skin flamed against his touch was almost unthinkable.

Except that he cared about her and they

were stuck in a weird space between needing to blow off steam and needing to be with each other. The former was a no-brainer. That's where Tyler existed most of the time. The latter scared the hell out of him.

Calling on every ounce of strength he had, he forced himself to slow it down a few notches.

The other side of the coin was that he realized she'd been through a lot and most likely needed an outlet for her stress. While that would normally be right up Tyler's alley, for reasons he couldn't explain it bothered him with Jessica.

"This is not a good idea right now." He lifted her up and set her on the bed next to him, doing his level best to squash the disappointment roaring through his chest and the little voice in the back of his mind cursing him out. That was the same piece of brain that controlled everything south and he'd learned as a teenager not to listen if he wanted to stay out of trouble.

"Oh" was all she said, and he could hear the surprise and disappointment clearly in her tone.

"You're beautiful, don't get me wrong. But anything happening between us is not going to work," he managed to say.

"It's okay. You don't have to spare my feelings." Her cheeks blushed and that ripped right through him.

Did she think he didn't want to have sex with her? How could he not? She had all the attributes he admired in a real woman. She was smart, had sexy curves and was damned near irresistible. In fact, if he didn't do something to cool his jets in the next minute or two he couldn't trust himself not to haul her into his arms again and take her right then and there on her bed. Before he went all caveman on her, he needed a cold shower. He'd explain later... when he figured it out for himself.

"We're going to talk about this, but not right now." He pointed at the phone. "First, we find your sister."

Before she could protest, he walked out of the room and straight into a cold shower.

IF THAT DIDN'T rank right up there as one of Jessica's most embarrassing moments in life, she didn't know what did. Clearly Tyler wanted her. There was no denying the erection she'd felt against the inside of her thigh. Was there something horribly wrong with her that he couldn't follow through on that desire? Maybe he'd finally realized what he was doing and decided to put a stop to it. Everything had happened so fast that Jessica got swept up in the moment. The attraction between them was real, but there was more to a relationship than physical pull. And he was right. They needed to focus on finding her sister.

Guilt washed over Jessica for losing focus. Jenn needed her and she'd gotten momentarily wrapped up with the handsome cowboy.

Shaking it off, she dressed in jeans and a cotton shirt. Throwing her hair in a ponytail she tried not to focus too much on where they were going. There'd be mosquitoes in the swamp. Alligators. Bacteria. And all sorts of creatures eager to feed off human flesh and blood.

And if thinking about that didn't give her pause, nothing would.

Then there were the people themselves to contend with…people who preferred life off the grid with no cell service or contact with the outside world.

She took a fortifying breath and turned toward the living room. Tyler stood there, dressed and fresh from a shower, staring.

"Ready?"

"As much as I'll ever be," she said, thoroughly confused by the mixed signal.

He picked his phone up from the bed and made a call.

"Who are you calling in the middle of the night?" she asked, slipping on her running shoes. If she was going to hike through the swamps in the middle of the night, then she figured that she'd need to be comfortable.

"It's not safe to drive around in Zander's limo anymore. I'm arranging transportation," he said.

"LET'S GIVE OUR eyes a few minutes to acclimate to the darkness before we head out." Tyler adjusted the seat of the SUV that had been organized for him by the hotel manager. He didn't normally play that card, the one that had him waking up a hotel manager in the middle of the night, but this felt like a real lead and waiting until morning could be the difference between life and death for Jessica's sister.

He'd also arranged for a flashlight but he wanted some peripheral vision as they made their way through dense woods to The Bayou.

"How far is it from here?" she asked.

"About twenty minutes on foot." He'd parked off the highway near the gravel road leading to the place. Any lights on that road would give them away and he didn't want anyone to know they were coming. He had no idea if The Bayou was a safe place or not. Given its coordinates, he couldn't imagine that it was...this was a place people went to fly off the radar. He grabbed a package of bug repellent wipes out of the bag he'd arranged to have in the vehicle, opened one and held it out. "Rub this on any exposed skin, neck, arms."

She took the wipe and her fingers grazed his palm. Again he regretted not following through with sex earlier. He still couldn't figure out what was wrong with him. The tension between them was a distraction they couldn't afford and he half figured a rousing round in the sack would help with that problem. Maybe then he could fully concentrate on finding Jenn instead of thinking about the curve of Jessica's sweet bottom in his hands.

Tyler tore open a packet of bug repellant and wiped his arms and neck. The last thing he needed was a case of West Nile to take home, and he sure as hell could use a distraction from thinking about Jessica's backside.

"We'll go in dark, meaning I'll cut off the flashlight when we get near the clearing to the building. If we're lucky, everyone on the premises will be asleep. If we're not, there'll be dogs and people with guns who will wake up when they bark. Based on the Google Earth picture, it looks like the kind of place there'd be Dobermans or pit bulls. So, not only will we go in dark but we'll go in quiet."

His eyes were adjusting to the darkness and hers were huge with fear.

"You want to wait it out here?" he asked, his voice more curt than he'd intended.

Her reaction was immediate. "No. I'd do more good with you and I'm not sitting out here alone."

He silently cursed at himself for not being able to stop thinking about their encounter in the hotel room. "You know how to handle a gun?"

"They scare me to death."

"Well," he conceded, "then we'll find something else for you to—"

"But that doesn't mean I can't get over it," she interrupted. "I'm not *that* afraid and especially if it means getting my sister to safety or keeping one of us from getting shot."

She held out her flat palm and he could see her hand tremble in the light of the full moon. He had to hand it to her. She got extra points for bravery.

"The safety is on." He molded her fingers around the SIG Sauer. "It's important to get a good feel for how it fits."

She brought her other hand up and cupped the butt. "I got this."

"You gave me the impression this was the first time you'd touched a gun."

"I said that I was scared to death of them, and that part's true, but my dad taught me how to shoot when I was twelve because he kept guns in the house."

"Was he a hunter?"

"No. We lived in a bad part of town and he wanted me to be ready in case he couldn't be around." She opened the magazine and checked the clip. "This should do but I'm hoping that I won't need to use it."

"Make sure it's aimed at someone besides me if you decide to shoot," he said, only half teasing. After his stunt back at the room she had to be angry with him. Heck, he was angry at himself. He still didn't know why a bout of conscience had come over him.

Taking a beautiful woman to bed didn't normally have him getting inside his head about not being in a relationship with her. *Damn, O'Brien.* He'd really loused that one up. If he got another chance with Jessica, and he was pretty sure that wasn't going to happen based on the wall she'd erected between them, he wouldn't waste it like he had the first time. But then second chances rarely happened in the real world. Tyler muttered a curse.

"What did you say?" she asked, looking at him oddly.

"Nothing." He hesitated. "Are you ready?"

"As much as I can be," she said softly, and her blatant honesty pierced his heart.

Yeah, he was going to live to regret his actions in the hotel. Because walking away from a woman with that much strength and beauty was going to be the end of him. But, hey, just like his short-lived baseball career and his last relationship had proved, everything had an expiration date.

Tyler tried to let this thing with Jessica roll off his back, ignoring the fact that it had more staying power than a determined bull on rodeo day.

THE SOUNDS OF a swamp in Louisiana at night were not something Jessica would ever get used to. There was a clicking sound to her right as she navigated the dense forest of live oak. Everything sounded alive, even the trees, and more awake than in daylight. Something rustled in the undergrowth a little too close for comfort and her heart skittered as she stepped over gnarled roots.

Crickets chirped, her skin crawled and the sound of footsteps slogging through muddy water sent her pulse racing. This was home of the alligator.

Owls hooted in surround sound and she could tell they were literally all around her as she stepped in the marsh. Something moved underneath her shoe. She bit back a scream and reached for Tyler.

He positioned her beside him and she kept her gaze focused on the light beam that hit a tree and then bounced to the ground and back. Step by step she held her breath, trying not to focus on the chorus of insects. Heaven only knew what other creatures were lurking in the dark. She couldn't help but check for a set of eyes as the light skimmed the deeper water right next to them and she prayed they wouldn't end up waist deep as they trudged along.

Who in their right mind would come out this far from the city and into this unknown? If her sister had been taken, and Jessica was fairly certain that was the case, then this would be the perfect place to dispose of a body.

Focusing on the worst-case scenario wouldn't help their investigation or her mood, so she did her best to shove those thoughts aside as she plucked her heel from the slick soil. It was impossible to move through the vegetation without making a sound. Every time she stepped, it was as if the ground refused to let go.

Tyler squeezed her hand and stopped. The light from the flashlight disappeared, plunging them into utter darkness.

Jessica's heart beat in her throat as she took a tentative step forward. Trust wasn't her strong suit but desperation had her willing to do pretty much anything to find her sister. The total blackness ignited her claustrophobia and if it wasn't for Tyler she would've had to stop right there and turn around.

If Jenn had been on her own she'd have called. There was no doubt about that in Jessica's mind. It had been two days since her sister had gone silent. A lot could happen in forty-eight hours.

Her eyes adjusted to the darkness enough to see outlines by the time the trees thinned. She counted three sheds and her sister could be in any one of them. Then there was the main building, a relatively small two-story structure with a handmade sign on the porch that read The Bayou in big white letters on what appeared to be a large piece of driftwood. That was about the only thing she could see clearly because the trees around the house formed a canopy in the swamp making it impossible for light from the moon to shine through.

Two vehicles were parked in back, an old Toyota pickup truck and a Volkswagen van that looked like a relic from the sixties. Thankfully, there were no dogs on the premises or

Jessica and Tyler's presence would already be known.

Tyler squatted down behind the Volkswagen and motioned for Jessica to come over. He flashed the light. The license plate on the VW read, Big Beau.

Jessica tried to wrap her mind around what this could mean. Her sister had mentioned The Bayou and then Elijah had referred to Big Beau. This had to be the place.

This could be a trap, a little voice said. Maybe she was right where Elijah wanted her.

Did that mean that Jenn was here somewhere?

Was this some kind of headquarters or meeting place for the group who was after the Infinity Sapphire?

A hand covered Jessica's mouth. Before she could scream she was dragged backward. She spun around out of her assailant's grasp, landed facedown and fumbled for the SIG Sauer she'd dropped in the struggle.

"Shhh. Don't scream. I'm here to help you and your sister. Don't say a word," the unfamiliar deep male voice said.

Tyler was there in the next beat, his gun at the man's temple. "Where do you think you're going with her?"

"Stay calm and we'll all get out of here alive," the man said.

From her vantage point, Tyler seemed the one in charge so it was bold of this guy to give orders. Her hand skimmed the surface of the ground until landing on her gun. She picked it up, sat up and pointed it directly at the male figure.

"I'm Big Beau. And if you want to know where your sister is, you'll keep quiet. We need to get out of here right now. If they know I'm talking to you I'll end up floating in that swamp. If the gators don't haul me off, the mosquitoes will."

"I have a car nearby," Tyler whispered.

She wasn't sure how Tyler knew to trust the guy. She had her own doubts, but desperation had her ready to do almost anything to find Jenn.

"Let's go before somebody wakes," Big Beau said. The guy was huge. Tyler was some-where around six foot four so he was signifi-cantly taller, but Big Beau had the belly of a grizzly bear.

"Not so fast." Tyler patted the guy down to check for a weapon as Jessica scrambled to her feet.

"You won't find anything on me. I left my AR15 inside and there's more where that came from. But if you're smart, you'll move it along. If we wake anyone up or they know I'm helping you, I'm dead. And so is Jenn."

Chapter Twelve

At the SUV, Tyler kept his gun leveled at Big Beau. Getting a closer look at him Jessica saw what a big, burly man he was. A patchwork of scruff covered parts of his jaw and neck. He wore a flannel shirt with the sleeves cut off. His eyes were pale blue, his hair dirty blond. Jeans rode low on his hips, tucked underneath a pot belly.

"I know what you're thinking and I ain't like them others," he said, holding his right hand toward Tyler as if it could stop a bullet.

"Prove it," Tyler shot back, keeping his gun aimed at the big guy. "Tell us where she is."

"She ain't far. Unless they've moved her."

"Who has her?" Jessica asked defensively.

"It's complicated but I remember you from the first time your sister brought you here," he said.

"How? That was so long ago. I don't remember you at all," she said honestly.

Big Beau held back a laugh. "Your sister came out here and talked about you all the time since then. I hoped you'd figure out she was in trouble and come see me."

"If that's true, then why doesn't anyone else know me?" She seriously doubted Jenn spoke about her to anyone.

He rolled his big shoulders in a shrug. "Reckon she had her reasons. She never talked about you where anyone else could hear and always asked me to keep it a secret."

"Because she was ashamed of me," Jessica said quietly. Then she glanced up apologetically. She hadn't intended to say that out loud.

"Ashamed?" He shook his head. "Proud's more like it. She went on and on about how smart you are and what a success you've made out of your family's business to help your parents."

"I had no idea she felt that way." True, she had expanded the cleaning business from houses to office buildings so her mother wouldn't have to do the heavy lifting anymore. And she'd hired two dozen workers, jobs she was happy to provide to people in order to boost the local economy.

Big Beau looked like he was examining Jessica and it made her uncomfortable. "I'm sorry for staring, but you two look so much alike. I'm surprised at how different you think or that you don't know how proud she is of you. She talks about you like you walk on water."

"Me and my sister have always been close but I didn't know." Jessica wiped an errant tear as it rolled down her cheek. She'd always loved her sister and had known on some level that Jenn loved her as much, but hearing that her sister was proud of her overwhelmed her with emotion.

"Jenn used to say all she had to work with was her looks," Big Beau continued. "And that she had to play her cards right or she'd end up with nothing. But you…she thought you hung the moon."

Jessica couldn't stop the sob that tore from her throat. Tyler moved to her side and put his arm around her protectively.

"I'm fine." She ignored the confused look on Tyler's face as she sidestepped out of reach. "Really. It's just very sweet to hear and my sister's in trouble. I let my emotions get the best of me but I'm good now."

Tyler eyed her up and down, clearly not convinced, but not ready to push the envelope either.

"Why didn't you do anything to help her?"

she asked Big Beau, needing to redirect the conversation to something more productive.

"It ain't right how they're setting her up to look like she stole that necklace. They plan to kill her as soon as they get hold of it and make it look like suicide. As far as helping her, that's what I'm trying to do right now."

"She's innocent?" Jessica knew she shouldn't sound so surprised. She wanted to believe in her sister, but after learning about the affair, it was hard. "Who's behind this?"

She was so close that he could reach out and grab her if he wanted, but she didn't care.

"Ashton Brasseux. But now that Randall Beauchamp's involved it's a mess," Beau said, and turned toward Tyler. "She's my friend and I wouldn't do anything to hurt her. My family don't feel the same way. Everyone's afraid of Mr. Beauchamp so they do whatever he asks. They don't have no trouble with her personally but he said to find her, so they did."

"What's Beauchamp's involvement in this?" Tyler asked.

Big Beau shrugged. "All I know is he has a buyer for that stolen necklace and now that it's gone missing he'll do anything to get it back."

"Is she hurt?" Jessica asked Big Beau. "Did he do anything to her?"

"I can tell you where I believe he's keeping

her, but that's as far as I can go. I have no idea what shape she's in. My guess is not good. If he knows anyone from my family helped you out he'll have us all fed to the gators." Big Beau shivered.

"But she's alive?" Jessica could barely ask the question.

"She was last I heard," he said honestly. "No way was she involved in this. Ashton used her."

That made a lot of sense.

"You can trust us. No one will know the information came from you," Tyler promised.

Big Beau half smiled and nodded. "My life depends on it."

"Why are you helping us?" Jessica asked.

"Your sister's a good kid." Big Beau's face broke into a smile talking about Jenn. She had that effect on people, and especially men. She was charming and beautiful, but there was something else about her that drew people to her. "She don't mean nobody harm. It's a shame what's happened to her and it's even worse that my family's to blame. I'll give you the address where we took her."

Big Beau relayed the coordinates of a place he said was in town.

"Elijah told us about you. He was trying to set a trap for us, wasn't he?" Jessica asked.

"He doesn't know Jenn and I are close, so I

figure he thought he was sending you to your demise. Nobody's going to find out you were here from me," Big Beau said. "Unless the gators start talking, I reckon no one will ever know."

He winked.

"Thank you." Jessica hugged Big Beau. Not because he would cover their tracks but because he cared about Jenn and had opened Jessica's eyes to a whole new side to her sister. Jenn had always come across as so confident, letting everything roll off her. Inside, she was far more fragile than Jessica realized and she wanted to protect her sister.

He seemed taken back by the gesture and stiffened. "Go on, now. Find Jenn and get her out of the state until this whole mess settles down."

"Do you know James Milton?" she asked.

"He that no-good lawyer she messed with last year?" Big Beau asked.

"He tried to kill me when he thought I was Jenn," she supplied.

"I reckon lots of folks want to get their hands on that missing necklace," Big Beau said, his anger evident on his face. "That's a stupid move, though. Everyone knows Beauchamp wants it."

"I thought he might be working for him."

"Doubt it. He could be trying to get in his good graces, though," Big Beau said. "Or pay off a debt."

"He's a gambler," she said, remembering the news they'd received from the sheriff.

"Well then, he might be trying to get himself out of trouble," Big Beau said.

"My sister sent me with him as a distraction. She wanted him out of town. You know anything about that?" she asked.

"Sure don't."

"What else do you know about my sister?"

"Not much. She liked to mix with men who wore shiny shoes and fine suits. Most of them hang in the same crowd and do a little too much sharing. She didn't like to be reminded that she was really just one of us," Big Beau said. "A man with shiny shoes usually has a slick tongue in my experience."

Jenn must've liked having some reminders of her past because she'd made friends with Big Beau. Jessica was less trustful of men in general and rich men in particular. She'd seen the way prominent men manipulated others. That was half the reason she stuck around to run the business she'd grown with her mother. Greed was powerful and she'd seen the damage firsthand.

"I best get back," Big Beau said. "Be careful who you trust. Folks around here have a way of knowing each other. Families, connections, they sometimes make no sense but go way back."

"We will," Jessica reassured him, as if she needed to be reminded there was no one she trusted besides Tyler and Big Beau.

Tyler set the coordinates in his phone as Jessica started toward the side of the SUV. She turned around to thank Big Beau once again but he wasn't there. He'd already disappeared into the bush. The thought of making that journey again sent a shiver down Jessica's spine.

TYLER HAD BEEN expecting another place near the swamps and was shocked when he pulled into an upscale family suburb with rows of white colonials. If Jenn was here, she was being held in plain sight.

"You sure this is the right area?" Red asked, echoing his sentiments.

"These are the coordinates." Tyler motioned to his phone, which had been giving the directions aloud.

Tyler's ringtone sounded. He pulled to the side of the road, turned off his lights and kept the engine idling. He glanced at the screen. "It's my brother, Austin." He answered the call. "Yo, what's up, Ivy League?" His second old-

est brother had gone to college in the north-
east, earning the nickname.

"Russ called me because you didn't show up
this morning," Austin said. His voice sounded
as though he'd only been awake a few minutes.
"Everything okay?"

Damn. Tyler had meant to touch base at the
ranch and ask someone to cover his area for the
next few days. "Yeah, fine. Had a last-minute
trip. Personal business."

"Lyndsey?"

An awkward tension filled the cab of the
SUV. "No. That's long finished."

"You sure about that?" Austin pressed.

Now was not the time to discuss her.

"Positive. That the only reason you called?"
Tyler didn't mean to sound defensive.

"Can a man check on his favorite brother?"
Austin scoffed, his sense of humor intact.
"This is what happens when people wake me
up before the sun comes out, by the way."

Tyler chuckled. Austin was no early riser.
"Yeah. I'm good, though. No need to worry
about me."

"Then I won't stress about the stranger
who's been asking around in town for Tyler
O'Brien," Austin said.

"You catch a name?" Tyler asked as Jessica shot him a concerned look.

"All I know is Tommy called and said you were helping out a woman who was in trouble. Next thing I know a stranger is looking for you and you're not showing up to work, which I don't have to say is unlike you," Austin said, more than a hint of curiosity in his tone.

"Janis didn't tell you that I'm out of town?" Tyler asked, thankful he'd remembered to talk to her. He wanted to tell his brother what was going on but needed to speak to Jessica about it first.

"It must've slipped her mind," Austin said.

"In her defense, I called after I left and never said I'd be gone long."

"Give Tommy a call when you can. He didn't sound himself," Austin said.

"I plan to touch base with him after breakfast." It wasn't a lie, even though Jessica shot him a cross look. She couldn't object to him bringing in Tommy after they found Jenn. Jessica's concern so far had been that whoever had her sister would kill her if the cops were chasing them. No one would get rid of her until they had that jewel.

"You hear about the Infinity Sapphire going missing?" Austin asked.

A pleading look came from the passenger seat. Jessica's hands folded into prayer position.

"I read something about it the other day." Playing dumb would only make Austin suspicious. He knew that Tyler read the newspaper every day, just as he did. They'd also had the Brasseuxs at the ranch, so Tyler would notice a story about the prominent family.

"I wondered about the Brasseuxs after the gala," Austin said.

"You did?" Tyler was shocked. He hadn't heard anything and his brother had been quiet up until now.

"I overheard him telling his wife that her spending was out of control," Austin said. "And then her necklace worth millions goes missing a couple months later."

"You think he was involved in an insurance scam?" Tyler wasn't sure if he should tell his brother that the Brasseuxs might be in trouble, but he was certain about that call to Tommy later. Maybe his friend had dug up more information.

"Who knows? The only thing I'm sure of is crossing them off the list for next year's gala." Austin chuckled and then paused when he didn't hear Tyler do the same.

Right. His comment was meant to be funny.

"You sure everything's okay?" Austin asked.

"Yeah. Why wouldn't it be?" Tyler tried to laugh it off. It was too much, too late but Austin didn't press.

"Get in touch with Tommy later. You have any idea when you'll be back at the ranch?" Austin asked.

"Couple of days should be enough to tie up a few loose ends here," Tyler said.

"I'll let everyone know." Austin paused. "Take care of yourself, brother. And call when you're ready to talk about it."

"I will." Tyler didn't like holding back from his family and the secrets were racking up. He ended the call and looked to Jessica. "Might be better to park here and walk to the end of the block."

The neighborhood had decent-sized yards and plenty of trees.

"Okay," Jessica said. She made a move for the door handle but stopped. "I'm sorry that you're lying to your family for me. I can tell how much it bothers you."

"It's—"

"Don't say that it's okay." Her hand came up in protest. "Because it's not fine for you to be dishonest with the people you love."

"I'd argue, but you're right. Austin understands and I didn't fool him for a second." He looked her in the eye. "And I need to make that call to Tommy later this morning. Right after we find your sister. I've thought this through and there's no reason not to tell him what's going on."

He really looked at her, expecting an argument.

"You're right. I want you to contact him as soon as we get my sister to safety," she said.

"He has no jurisdiction here, so whatever we're about to get ourselves into we're on our own anyway."

She nodded and brushed her hand against his arm. "Thank you for taking this risk for my family. If you want out, though, I'd totally understand."

"We've come too far for me to walk away now." He was rewarded with a small smile—it was sweet and sexy at the same time.

There was very little security at the house. Tyler didn't want to tell Jessica his real fear, that none was necessary because Jenn wasn't perceived as a threat. She would be immobilized and he had no idea what physical condition she'd be in when they found her. He was prepared to carry her over his shoulder for the mile and a half walk to his SUV if that's what it took.

The sun would be up soon, so they had to move fast.

Tyler wished there was a way to prepare Jessica, to soften the blow of seeing her sister in such a vulnerable state as they closed the distance between the tree line and the house.

They could go in through the raised basement. Tyler pulled his gun and motioned for Jessica to do the same. He walked policeman-style, gun and flashlight drawn, down a half dozen stairs.

The door was locked but he'd had enough experience with barn doors to figure out how to pick it.

Inside, the place was dark and dingy, and the floor slanted downward, resulting in water pooling in one corner of the space. Tyler immediately looked for alternate exits in case the cellar door was no longer an option. An old wall that divided the space was half-torn down. The stairs leading to the main floor were old and wooden. There would be people up there. They couldn't go out that way.

Tyler scanned the room for any signs of life. A woman sat crumpled over in a corner of the room. Her head was slumped to one side, her neck at an odd angle and for a split second Tyler feared the worst.

Jessica let out a little gasp before seeming to catch herself and going silent as she hurried over. She dropped down next to the woman and cradled her face. "Jenn."

Chapter Thirteen

Tyler took a knee on the other side of Jenn and checked for a pulse. Relief washed over him when he got one. "She's alive."

Jenn's eyes fluttered open and she immediately drew back. A cut ran down the side of her left cheek and her right eye was swollen and bruised.

"Don't be scared. It's me. I'm taking you home," Jessica said soothingly.

It took a minute for Jenn's eyes to focus, but when they did she scrambled toward Jessica, hugging her sister around the neck. She was aware and that was a good thing.

Tyler glanced around the room. He was a little surprised they'd left her alone in the basement. The lock on the cellar door had been easy enough to pick. This was an upper class suburban neighborhood and they must not figure that anyone would tie this place to criminal activity. It was the kind of place where he half expected to find a grandma upstairs, having risen early and gathered vegetables to begin preparing the roux that would cook all day until used in a dish such as crawfish étouffée for supper.

"I'm going to pick you up and take you out of here," Tyler said.

Jenn pulled back, fearful, and shook her head. Her lips were dry, cracked and he wondered how long it had been since she'd had water. Getting her hydrated would be his first priority as soon as he got her out of there.

"It's okay, sweetie. This is my friend and he's here to help," Jessica said, her voice rising in panic. "What's wrong?"

Jenn shifted her position to reveal her ankles. Her feet had been tucked underneath her bottom so they'd missed the thick ropes around her ankles. Tyler followed the bindings to a three-inch PVC pipe climbing up the wall that disappeared into a hole in the ceiling. He pulled out his cell.

"What are you doing?" Jessica asked, placing her hand on his arm.

"Calling the police."

Jenn shook her head again and Tyler stopped, his finger hovering over the nine.

"I have no choice. I can't take a chance and I

sure as hell can't leave you like this. We make any noise down here and I guarantee the room will fill with more men with guns than you can shake a stick at. What else do you think we should do?" he asked.

"I loved him," Jenn managed to say, her voice raspy and she sounded so tired. "Get the necklace. Keep it safe."

"Or we get you out of here, find the necklace together, and then go to police," Tyler said, using a tone that said he was done talking.

"No police. Not yet," Jenn insisted. "Not while it looks like I did this. Who would believe that I'm innocent?"

She had a good point. Currently, evidence pointed directly at her involvement.

"The truth will come out," Jessica soothed her sister. She was putting up a brave front but it was clear to Tyler that she was fighting to keep her emotions in check. "All anyone would have to do is look at you to know you're innocent."

"I go to the police and I'm dead," Jenn said, and it looked like it took an incredible amount of effort to speak.

Her statement was true and he couldn't deny it. She was afraid for good reason. Tyler tucked his phone into his pocket.

"Then we find a way to get you out of here

and figure this out," Jessica said emphatically, obviously not wanting to upset her sister with the information about Elijah and Milton. "But I am not leaving you here. Do you understand me? I won't do it."

Tyler slid his arm around Jessica's waist, trying to soothe her.

She smiled up at him and then scooted closer to her sister and out of his reach.

"Where's Ashton?" Jenn whispered. It was barely loud enough for Tyler to hear.

"I don't know," Jessica said.

Tyler searched the space for something he could use to cut the rope. Seeing Jenn like this, defenseless and in a basement, he understood why they didn't think they'd need security and this was just what he'd feared. They were hiding her in plain sight and were confident...too confident?

Even so, the move was pretty brilliant if anyone asked Tyler, and he'd have to keep that in mind moving forward. These guys were clever career criminals and neither Jenn nor Jessica would be safe until those men were locked behind bars.

There was nothing around to use to free Jenn. The sun would be up soon. That meant someone would most likely be down to check on her.

Old houses were notorious for having pipes that ran nowhere. Was it possible that the PVC pipe she was attached to would be the same? He stood and ran his fingers as high as he could reach on the PVC pipe. The ceiling wasn't more than seven feet high so he could reach fairly far into the ceiling. He curled his index finger around the end of the pipe. Jackpot.

Tyler twisted the pipe but it wouldn't budge. There was probably twenty years of grime holding it together. He clamped his back teeth together and gave another twist, netting a little movement this time. Digging deep, he squeezed the pipe and turned. This time, it gave. He pulled apart the pipes by threading one through the ceiling. They could worry about the ropes later. His first priority was getting her out of there. He scooped her off the floor and raced toward the cellar door.

Jessica went first, pushing through the door and into the beginnings of sunlight.

Two men in an SUV with dark windows burst from the vehicle. Tyler cursed and he heard Jessica do the same. They must've been reporting to work because they hadn't been there fifteen minutes ago.

"Run and keep running. No matter what happens," he said, figuring they still had a chance if Jessica could get away. She would have to call the police then. Of course, with criminals this smart, he and Jenn would be hidden in a new location.

Tyler had no intention of going down without a fight.

"Stop," one of the men shouted.

Tyler didn't look back. He ran on burning legs. At this distance, the men would have to be spot-on shots to hit him, although he liked his odds less since he was a good-sized target. Once he got to the trees, *if* he got to the trees, it would be even more difficult for them to get off an accurate shot. They could circle back to their SUV once they got away from the men. Try running there now and the men would catch them before they could get Jenn inside.

He could get to the trees, but then what? If he could set Jenn down, turn around and pull out his gun in time then maybe he could hold them off.

Carrying roughly a hundred and twenty pounds of woman put him at a distinct disadvantage. He chanced a glance behind. The men were closing in fast.

The trees were too far and he realized that there was no way he was going to make it in time. Either of the men could stop and fire at this point and have a good chance at hitting him. His best guess as to why they hadn't fired already was that they wanted Jenn alive because they assumed she knew where the necklace was hidden.

All his and Jessica's efforts to save Jenn wouldn't matter the second these guys caught up with them. He couldn't outrun them and he could hear their footsteps closing in.

The next second, Jessica spun around with her gun leveled. "Duck."

Tyler dropped to the ground, holding on to Jenn, whose arms were wrapped so tightly around his neck she was almost cutting off his ability to breathe.

A bullet split the air, Jenn screamed and Tyler half feared she'd been shot by mistake. He looked behind him to see the men had scattered in the opposite direction, running for cover. His chest shouldn't fill with pride for Jessica's quick thinking but it did. And he was darn grateful she wasn't a lousy shot or he might've ended up with a bullet in his skull.

He popped to his feet and blazed past her. "Let's go."

Only when they were deep in the woods and there was no sign of pursuit did he feel it was safe to stop and catch his breath. "Way to think on your feet back there."

Jessica smiled and it quickly faded as she

put her arm around her sister. "I can't take her home. That's the first place they'll look. I have to figure out a way to warn our parents without telling them what's going on. And we need to stay out of sight until we sort this out."

Tyler waited for his breathing to slow before talking. "I can make sure your family is safe. I'll send someone to pick them up and take them away for an extended vacation. And I have the perfect place to hide while we figure this out. There are blind spots on my ranch and I know just where they are. We can pitch a tent on my land and stay under the radar."

"She's too weak and she needs medical care," Jessica said. "And these guys won't let up."

"I have other plans for her and those men with guns are exactly the reason we need to find a place to hunker down for a few days and give her time to recoup. She needs medical care and I know where she can get it and still be safe." He examined the cut on Jenn's face. "All the wounds are superficial so they'll heal quickly as long as there's no infection. In the meantime, I'd put money on the fact that necklace has to be somewhere in Texas and I'm betting it's near Bluff."

"Of course, that's why Milton believed me and took me there," Jessica said. "I guess he figured he'd get me to tell him where it was and then he'd take it back himself. And then he could collect a reward from Mr. Beauchamp or use it to get in his good graces."

"Gambling" was all Jenn managed to say. She needed water, food and a day's worth of rest before she could say much more. Nearly three days of who knew what conditions she'd been in other than the basement. The only good news was that she seemed otherwise healthy and should bounce back given a little time to recoup.

"What did you say?" Jessica asked, leaning closer.

"She said gambling. I'm guessing Milton's trouble had to do with a betting addiction," Tyler said.

Jenn nodded.

"But you didn't think he'd turn on you," Tyler clarified.

"No." A look of horror crossed Jenn's weary features as she looked at her sister. "I would never have—"

"I know. Don't try to talk right now. It's okay," Jessica soothed. "I know you would never put me in danger on purpose."

"We need to stay on the move," Tyler said as he moved toward Jenn. "And get her into the SUV."

He scooped her up and she wrapped her arms around his neck again. He'd rather go straight to Tommy than to the ranch. There was no doubt that Tyler could trust his long-time family friend. Jessica and Jenn seemed to have other ideas. He needed to help them see the light.

So far the only thing the three of them agreed on was getting Jenn out of the state and keeping her off the radar while she gained her strength. But Tyler had every intention of calling his friend. Jessica had green-lighted the connection before and nothing in their present circumstance changed his mind.

THE FLIGHT HOME was smooth as the morning sun settled in the sky. Jessica was grateful to have her sister back. During the flight she'd racked her brain to put the pieces together. Milton had obviously been in some kind of gambling trouble and when Jessica couldn't deliver the necklace, he'd tried to kill her, believing her to be Jenn.

Jessica had an endless list of questions… would Elijah realize Big Beau had allegiance to Jenn now that she'd escaped? Elijah had figured Jessica out. But who stole the necklace in the first place?

Everyone seemed to believe that Jenn knew

where this multi-million-dollar necklace was, but she was too weak to talk. Answers would have to wait until she was hydrated and feeling better.

"Checked the weather in Bluff before we took off," Tyler said, interrupting her hamster-wheel of questions. "It should be in the low sixties for the next few days. Perfect camping weather."

Images of the last time she was on his land flashed through her thoughts. Of turning to find Milton standing there, rock in hand, ready to bash her head in. That image was burned into her brain.

After settling the airplane in the hanger, Tyler helped Jenn into the backseat of his SUV. She was moving a little better now that he'd removed the ropes from her ankles. He'd given her ibuprofen and water from his emergency kit and Jenn had slept during the flight home.

Jessica was grateful for Tyler. She couldn't imagine doing any of this alone—and yet hadn't she been alone her entire life? Sure, she'd had her sister and her parents, all people who leaned on her, but who did she have to depend on?

Without the Texas cowboy she had no idea where she would've ended up. Dead, she thought. She would've died if she'd been left underneath that ATV. A wild animal would've gotten to her or she would've wandered around on the property, lost, until she succumbed to dehydration or, if she'd survived long enough, starvation. The important thing was that she and Jenn were together and her sister would be okay.

Tyler took a call, walking around to the back of his SUV out of earshot. A pang of jealousy tore through her, which was silly. She had no designs on the cowboy, even though the few kisses they'd shared in the past twenty-four hours had left a piece of her thinking otherwise. Dating hadn't been a priority of late and especially since Brent. It was more than his infidelity that pierced her chest. It was the fact that she'd so easily given her trust to him, and how willingly he'd stomped all over it. Was she that bad a judge of character?

It would seem so, because she'd misjudged her sister, as well. It had taken a stranger, Big Beau, to tell Jessica what she really meant to Jenn.

How strange was that?

"That was my brother Dallas. Someone in a suit is still asking around for me in town," Tyler said, rounding the SUV to where she was sitting in the passenger seat with the door open.

"Why would they want you?" Then it must've

dawned on her. "They must've figured out that you were helping me."

"When your sister wakes up, we need to talk to her."

"Do you think she'll be safe with us?" she asked. "I'm worried about her. She's been mumbling something and I think she's out of it."

"I was planning to call Dr. McConnell to have Jenn examined. We could check her into the hospital under a fake name. I can send security to keep an eye on her 24/7 while we continue to investigate. I'm certain the doc will accommodate us without asking a lot of questions."

Jessica chewed on that thought for a minute. She liked the idea of having her sister in a facility where she could be properly cared for. Looking at her in this condition was a cause for serious stress. Would Jenn fight them on it? Could she? As it was, she could barely lift her head and her ramblings were becoming more frequent and less distinguishable.

"She'll get well faster in a place she can be looked after properly," he said with a convincing look.

"Okay. Let's do that. If we can get her to agree," she said.

"Her eyes have barely opened since Baton

Rouge. I doubt she has any fight left inside her." Tyler had a point. He walked away, presumably to give her time to think about it.

Jessica looked in the backseat. Her sister was resting comfortably but she needed medical care in order to get better. What if infection set in or she was bleeding internally? She already favored her right side, moving carefully as if one of her ribs was broken. She needed X-rays and an IV.

But that would mean leaving her in the hospital.

The thought of not staying with Jenn hit Jessica like a two-by-four to the chest. But what choice did she have? It wasn't like Jenn was waking up. She could have a concussion or worse. Even though Jessica couldn't imagine walking away from her sister, she wouldn't deny her medical service or put her in danger because of her selfishness.

Fighting tears, she walked over to where Tyler stood forty feet away. No way was she going to let the handsome cowboy see her cry again. This was the right thing to do for her sister. "Signing my sister into the hospital under an assumed name is the best way to go. Can you arrange it?"

Tyler took her hand in his and tugged her toward him. She leaned into his strong chest and he wrapped his arms around her. And in that moment, crazy as it might sound, she felt safe.

"You're making the right call. She'll be well cared for in the hospital and it's the last place Milton or anyone else will look since you've already been there."

She nodded. "Plain sight."

"That's right," Tyler said. "I'll call Dr. McConnell and set everything up."

Jessica wiped a rogue tear. "It's hard to see her like this. She's normally so strong and willful."

"We'll get her the care she needs and you'll be back to your twin antics in a few days," he said, an obvious attempt to make her smile.

It worked.

Chapter Fourteen

Tyler pulled off the highway and then around the back of the Quick Gas Auto Mart on the outskirts of town where an ambulance waited. Dr. McConnell had insisted this would be the best and safest way to transport Jenn to the hospital, and he figured she was right on both counts.

Jenn could begin receiving fluids immediately and, given that she was severely dehydrated, that should make a big difference in her general health. Glancing at Jessica as he parked had him wondering if she would be able to walk away from her sister. Agony darkened her features and she was chewing on her thumbnail.

"They're going to take good care of Jenn and the doc said she'd call the minute your sister wakes up and is ready to talk," he said to reassure her, hoping she wouldn't change her mind at the last minute.

"You're right," she conceded. "It's just hard to leave her again."

Tyler waved the EMTs over. Andy and Shanks greeted Tyler as they went right to work helping Jenn out of the SUV and positioning her on the gurney.

Jessica was at her sister's side as Jenn's eyes fluttered open again.

"You're going to the hospital," Jessica said.

Jenn barely nodded.

"Everything's going to be okay and I'll see you very soon," Jessica reassured, rubbing her sister's arm.

Jenn opened her mouth to speak but looked as though she lost the energy. She took in a ragged breath and mouthed, *Love you*.

"Love you," Jessica parroted.

"We'll take good care of her, man, I promise," Shanks said to Tyler, looking from Jessica to Jenn. Tyler could almost see the question mark in his mind at the resemblance between the two.

Tyler patted Shanks on the back. "I know you will. And we'd appreciate it if you kept my involvement between us for now. In fact, if you could keep quiet about this whole thing."

"Doc mentioned something about this being

tied to a criminal case and her being a witness, but that's all she could say." Andy's eyes got wide and sparkly with excitement. He lowered his tone when he said, "Is she going into the witness protection program or something?"

"I'd like to tell you more but I'm sworn to silence," Tyler said, trying to sound disappointed. He didn't want to quell Andy's excitement, and figured his response would serve as a good reminder of how top secret this had to be.

"Right-o." Andy nodded and wheeled the gurney to the back of the ambulance with a satisfied smile.

As soon as Jenn was out of sight, tears started rolling down Jessica's face. Tyler glanced around, feeling exposed in their current location. He hugged her before ushering her into the SUV.

"Why do I feel like I'm never going to see her again?" Jessica said, wiping the tears from her face as she apologized. "I'm sorry. I'm not usually a crier."

"Never say you're sorry for showing your emotions," he said. Tyler had been an expert at stuffing his below the surface for too many years.

"I've always been the strong one, you know. It's why my sister always comes to me and this makes me feel weak." She motioned toward a rogue tear sliding down her cheek.

"Crying doesn't make you any less strong. Tears are just saltwater. The ocean is filled with it and that doesn't take away from its magnitude. Real strength means pushing through your boundaries when you're afraid and never giving up. Trust me when I say you have that in spades."

She smiled through red-rimmed eyes. "Thank you."

Tyler started the engine and navigated onto the highway, heading home. His heart fisted in his chest. He was in trouble. And this time, going home had a new meaning. Rather than rack his brain trying to crack that nut, he fisted the steering wheel and focused on something that made sense…the road in front of him.

"You're quiet all of a sudden," Jessica said.

"I just have a lot on my mind." It was partially true. Tyler couldn't stop thinking about Jessica and wasn't it his trick to shut down emotionally when he got close to someone or something he wanted? But then he hadn't wanted anything like he wanted her in his life and it confused the hell out of him.

Another thing he didn't want to think about right then.

Tyler decided to take her to the easternmost

tip of the property, furthest from his house, where people would least expect him to be. His SUV was made for off-roading and he'd need it to reach the location. The drive took another two hours. Jessica leaned her seat back and rested for the ride. He almost woke her half a dozen times to tell her that he was confused and wanted to sort out what was going on in his mind, but he stopped himself. She needed the rest and he liked having her there.

"This location will be out of the way for most of the ranch business and should keep us flying under the radar," he said when she finally sat up.

Pitching a tent didn't take long. He'd decided on camping next to Hollow's Lake, figuring they'd need a water source if they were going to be out there for a few days. This land wasn't near where they kept the cattle and therefore no one would be riding fences. There were no hunts scheduled on this side of the property in the month of November, so unless something had changed they'd be good. He had cursory supplies, including toiletries, in his SUV at all times in case he wanted to spend the night out on the range and sleep under the stars, which had happened often since hearing the news about his parents.

He built a campfire and offered Jessica a protein bar before making coffee.

"I'm impressed," she said, taking a sip.

"What you're tasting is the result of years of trial and error." He laughed.

"It's even more than that," she said, and he knew exactly what she was talking about. "What is it about a beautiful landscape that makes everything taste so much better?"

"Fresh air does something to food and drink."

She nodded. "Thank you for taking care of my sister."

"No problem," he said, but he could see that it was a huge deal to her.

JESSICA DIDN'T WANT to like the handsome cowboy any more than she already did. As soon as they figured out who was behind this crime and could prove it to the law she'd go back to Shreveport and running the family business so she could resume taking care of her parents. The thought made her sad. Not the part about taking care of her parents, but returning to Shreveport. The place no longer felt like home and the job had never before felt so lonely.

Could she convince Jenn to come home? Jenn? Come home?

Jessica almost laughed out loud. Her sister

hadn't been able to wait to get out of Shreveport. If Baton Rouge was no longer an option, and Jessica was pretty sure it wasn't, then maybe Jenn could get a fresh start in Houston or San Antonio.

Thinking about her sister brought on too much sadness, so she pushed those unproductive thoughts aside for now and tried to clear her head with another sip of coffee. They needed to figure out why Jenn was being set up.

"Have you heard from Zander?" she asked.

"He was released from the hospital last night and is doing fine." He sat staring with his back to the sun.

Had a wall come up between them? When Jessica really thought about it, Tyler clammed up every time they got close. What was that all about? He had feelings for her, or at the very least an attraction, and yet he shut down every time they tried to act on it. She made a mental note to ask him about it. Maybe it had something to do with his past.

"Did you really play pro baseball?" she asked, remembering a conversation with Zander.

"Yep."

"And what happened?"

"Nothing." He rubbed his right shoulder, a

move she'd seen him make several times when they'd done something physical.

"Everything okay?" She motioned toward the spot where his hand was rubbing.

He stopped midrub. "Peachy."

She pushed to her feet, unsure what she'd done to make him stop talking to her. All of a sudden they were at one-word answers and he looked uncomfortable. "I'm going for a walk."

"You want company?"

"No." What had happened? One minute he was comforting her and now they were barely speaking. What was up with that?

Jessica pushed those thoughts aside as she walked toward the lake. Every step away from Tyler was a giant leap toward being completely stressed. How had she become so dependent on a stranger in just a few short days?

Anger and frustration formed a tight ball in her chest, making breathing hurt. She had no right to feel this way about him and she needed to walk it off. Heck, she didn't want to feel this way about any man. And yet she couldn't deny that was exactly what was happening.

So the handsome cowboy had done a few nice things for her. Let's face it, his actions were nothing short of heroic. But that didn't mean she had to put up with his roller-coaster emotions—one minute on and the next keeping her at a safe distance.

At least this was better than her relationship with Brent. He'd been practiced and cool the whole time. He knew exactly the right words to say to throw her off the trail if she was suspicious…and it had all been one big act so she wouldn't catch him cheating.

Jessica paced from a mesquite tree to the lake's edge a few times before she looked up and realized that Tyler was standing right there watching her. She let out a little yelp before she could quash it. "What are you doing sneaking up on me like that?"

"I'm sorry." His wry grin belied the sincerity in those words.

"Great. The man *can* put two words together," she quipped and then regretted saying what she was thinking. She should probably bow at the man's feet for how much he was helping her family, so why did she want to claw his eyes out right now instead?

There he stood, silent, for a long moment with his arms crossed as he leaned against a tree.

Jessica would be damned if she spoke first. Two could play at that game, so she planted her fisted hands on her hips and stared right back.

"You want to scream or something? Go

ahead. No one will hear you out here," he said, as if he dared her to.

His stance was casual. Hers was aggressive. *Well, get used to it, buddy.* She had no plans to back down from a challenge.

"I would if it would help," she shot back. "Can't see how that'll make it easier to be around you, though."

"*I'm* the problem?" He almost sounded sincere but damned if that grin wasn't plastered into place on his face. It was sexy, she had to give him that, but a little sexy—okay a lot sexy!—wasn't about to make her cave. Besides, she was getting whiplash from his mood swings. One minute his hands were all over her, making her want things she hadn't felt before. And then the next he couldn't put enough distance or a bigger wall between them.

"Glad you see this from my point of view," she said, knowing full well his was a question not a statement. Well, he'd put it out there.

The smile faded from his lips and his hand flew behind his back at a sound behind her. "Get down."

She dropped to all fours at the exact time his gun came around and leveled at a spot where her head had been seconds before. A bullet cracked the air as fire flared from the tip of his barrel.

"Stay down," Tyler said, already on the move.

Jessica pulled her gun and crouched behind the tree where Tyler had been a few moments before, hoping to get a look at what he'd seen. She scanned the area next to the lake, the direction he'd fired, and couldn't see anyone. And now that it was getting dark, she'd lost sight of Tyler in the trees.

If anyone came near her, she'd have no qualms about shooting.

A few shots were fired at least forty feet away. She whirled toward the sound, trying to keep her hands from shaking as she gripped the gun and kept alert.

Rustling noises came from the same direction. Rather than move into the dangerous area, she maintained position. She wanted to call out to Tyler but did not want to compromise his position or hers. A thought crossed her mind. She was crouched in the spot from which he'd fired a few minutes ago. Her position was already compromised. She needed to move.

Staying low, she crawled toward the water.

It was eerie how everything had gone quiet.

Jessica sat near the water's edge, looking at her reflection in the moonlight. Still no sign of movement around her.

She completely stilled, quiet, for several minutes that dripped by like hours.

A hand touched her shoulder at the same time as he spoke. "It's okay."

She nearly jumped out of her skin. Using the momentum, she spun around on him. "It most certainly is not. I could've shot you."

That wry grin parted his lips. "You're not fast enough."

She let that slide, ignoring the sour taste in her mouth that came with knowing he was right.

Chapter Fifteen

"What happened? Who were you shooting at?" Jessica asked, trying to calm her fried nerves.

"I saw movement in the bush and something charged toward me. Turned out to be a wild hog," he said.

Tyler O'Brien was no doubt capable of handling any situation he came across, but Jessica couldn't ignore the fact that the cowboy lit up more of her senses than was good for either one of them.

Another noise sounded behind her. Jessica jumped and scrambled into his arms.

"Don't tell me you're afraid of a hog?" he asked, leaning back to get a better look at her.

"You're not?" she asked.

"They're mean but, trust me, I can be worse. I'm not going to let anything happen to you," he said and his voice was gravelly. "But *this* isn't a good idea."

"What?" she asked, but she was being coy. "Is *this*?" She reached up on her tiptoes and pressed a light kiss to his lips. Sure, she was frustrated with him and she figured half the reason their frustrations had built to this degree was all the sexual tension crackling around them every time he got near her. It was crazy and impulsive but all she could think about was the feel of his arms around her and how right everything felt when she was this close to him.

His heart thundered against her chest, its rhythm matching hers.

He closed his eyes and took a deep breath. "I can't stop whatever's going on between us and it scares the hell out of me."

"You don't have to be in control all of the time," she countered. "Maybe it's time we both let go."

With that, he closed his arms around her and pressed her body flush with his.

"I'm glad you feel that way, because this thing between us seems to have a mind of its own," he said. "I'm tired of fighting it."

A trill of need blasted through Jessica. "Those are the best words I've heard all day."

He dipped his head and claimed her mouth. She parted her lips and his tongue slid inside, tasting her, needing her.

Tyler picked her up and carried her to the tent. He set her down long enough to pull the sleeping bag outside, under the stars.

She shrugged out of her shirt, dropping it onto the ground, and he groaned when he saw her blue lace bra.

All it took was one step for him to be there, his hands on her breasts as her nipples beaded beneath the silk undergarment. He paused long enough to look into her eyes and she was certain he was searching for reassurance.

No words were needed as she tugged at the hem of his shirt. His joined hers on the ground a moment later and then his lips were on her neck, slowly moving down. He stopped at the heartbeat at the base of her neck, feathering little kisses there, and then slicked his tongue down the line between her breasts.

Her breath came out in little gasps as he explored her sensitized skin. She planted her hands firmly on either side of his shoulders to stop him.

"What? What's wrong?" he asked, and his voice was low.

"We're wearing too many clothes," she said, already grabbing for his zipper.

He shimmied out of his jeans and she did the same. Her bra came off a few seconds later and joined the other clothes on the ground.

Tyler stopped, his eyes dark and hungry, and looked at her. "You're beautiful."

"So are you," she said, tracing a line down the muscles in his chest. He was like touching silk over steel, raw power in physical form.

His hands roamed her breasts and she liked the rough feel of his fingers on her skin.

Her breath caught as he slipped her matching blue silk-and-lace panties down the sides of her hips with achingly slow movements.

She tugged his boxers off next and took a second to admire his glorious body in the moonlight. He was muscle and hotness with just the right amount of gruffness to be irresistibly sexy…damn. There was so much more to Tyler O'Brien than a hot body, although he had that in spades. He was warm, intelligent and caring…a potent combination. And she was hooked.

When this was all over and he walked away, the pain was going to be beyond anything she'd ever known…but she had tonight. And a little part of her mind told her she'd held back too long. She needed to take what she wanted… and she wanted the hot cowboy. Hurt would eventually heal and she would have this memory for the rest of her life.

Jessica made a move toward Tyler but he stopped her.

"I'm not done looking at you," he warned, naked and glorious.

She should be embarrassed but there was something about his presence that made her feel completely at ease. She glanced down at the makeshift bed on the ground, smiled, and then took off running in the other direction, straight to the water.

The cool lake practically sizzled against her burning skin.

Tyler was behind her in the next moment, spinning her to face him. She wrapped her legs around his waist and eased him inside her.

"You're going to destroy me," he said, his muscles taut as he thrust deeper inside her.

"In the best possible way," she said. "Now shut up and kiss me."

He did kiss her, his tongue thrusting inside her mouth as he filled her with his erection. One hand splayed against her bottom, the other pressed and tugged at one nipple then the other until she shattered into a thousand tiny pieces around him.

And then he detonated inside her as they, bare-naked skin to bare-naked skin, held each other in the moonlight.

TYLER WOKE BEFORE light peeked over the horizon, feeling a little too refreshed. There was a chill in the air that didn't penetrate his warm body—warm because of the woman in his arms. And a big part of him wanted to stay right there and hold her for as long as he could.

Good news about Jenn's condition would be a welcome relief for Jessica and he wanted to deliver it first thing. He needed to move to a spot on the north corner of the lake where he could check his cell phone.

Slowly, so he wouldn't wake her, he untangled their arms and legs with a satisfied smile. Last night had been right up there with…no, had been *the* best sex of his life.

When they sorted out Red's situation they needed to have a conversation about seeing each other on a regular basis, explore where this could go. He picked a few supplies out of his pack and moved to the water. After brushing his teeth, he replaced the supplies and hiked to the other side of the lake.

His first phone call would be to Dr. McConnell. It was early but she'd be up making rounds. He walked along the lake, checking various spots for bars until he got at least three. Immediately his cell phone started buzzing and dinging. Fifteen missed calls and a half dozen text messages. Not good.

The first was from the doc. She was direct,

as usual, saying that hospital security had been breached and her patient had gone missing.

Tyler immediately phoned.

"It happened an hour ago," she said, not bothering wasting time on perfunctory greetings. "I had to call the sheriff."

That second statement was a given. Jessica might be upset at first but she'd see that the doc had no choice.

"What did Tommy say?" he asked.

"He figured it was connected to the murder at the motel. I didn't link you to my patient. That's between you and Tommy," she said.

"What was her condition?" Jessica needed to know what they were dealing with. "Tell me in layman's terms."

"She'd had two bags of saline, so she was rehydrating. Overall, I've seen worse but I don't like her being gone before I had a chance to evaluate all her injuries." The doctor hesitated for a second. "How's her sister?"

"What gave her away?" Tyler asked.

"She doesn't have the same bruising on her arms, for one," Dr. McConnell said. "That was the first tell."

He should've known. "I apologize for not being up front. This situation is sticky and some information wasn't mine to share."

"You have your reasons," she said quickly.

"I've known you a long time and I trust they're good ones."

He thanked her and asked if he could see the security footage.

"I'll have someone drop a copy of the feed off at the ranch," she said. "It would be best if you stayed away from here for now."

"Understood."

"On that note, the images are grainy. We don't have a need for high-tech security here so the equipment's old," she said.

"How many people are we talking here?" he asked, hoping to get a better frame around who they might be dealing with.

"Just one," she said, and there was an ominous quality to her tone.

"Did you recognize him, by chance?" he asked.

"I'd swear it was the man visiting her sister the other day."

James Milton.

"I better get ahold of Tommy and see what he's found so far." And he needed to come clean to his close friend. The best way to help Red and her sister was to lay all the cards on the table. On second thought, he'd shoot a text asking Tommy to meet at the cabin. It would be easier to explain everything with Red there.

"I'm here if you need anything," Dr. McConnell said.

"We'll be out of cell range for a bit this morning. You hear anything or if anyone connected to this shows up at the hospital, I'd appreciate a heads-up."

"Already have you on speed dial." She paused. "At the risk of sounding motherly, be careful."

"You know I will," he said before ending the call.

Tyler made a beeline toward the tent. Jenn had gone missing and Milton had her. Tyler had miscalculated the man and her disappearance was on his head.

Jessica needed to know.

Chapter Sixteen

Tyler didn't like the idea of waking Red before she'd had a chance to get a proper night's rest, but this news couldn't wait. They needed to regroup and come up with a plan to find her sister, now. "I have news."

She blinked her eyes open.

"We need to talk," he said, kissing her on the forehead.

Red sat up, yawned and rubbed her eyes. "What's up?"

Bad news got worse with age so he didn't wait for the right words to come. "A man breached hospital security an hour ago and managed to get away with your sister."

The look of shock and horror playing out on her face fisted his chest. He'd let her down in the worst possible way.

"Who? How?" she asked, wide-eyed.

"I can't say for certain. Dr. McConnell is

sending security films to the house. If we pack up now we should be there around the same time." Tyler was already gathering supplies. "She was doing better because she was getting hydrated, but doc said she didn't get a chance to get a full workup yet."

"And, let me guess, they have no idea who took her?" she asked again.

He looked her directly in the eyes. "Doc's pretty certain it was James Milton."

Panic crossed her features as she scrambled to her feet. "What do we need to do?"

"Pack up and go home."

Within ten minutes, the campfire had been tamped, the SUV packed and they were on the road. Tyler drove across the property, calling ahead to security to alert them he was coming. His next call was to his brother Austin.

"We have a situation and need to send out an alert to security," Tyler said as soon as his brother answered. "The woman I've been helping, Jessica, her sister is missing and they're both in danger. Everyone should stay vigilant and be on the lookout for Jessica's twin sister and a white male. If people want a visual, I'll be at my place in the next twenty minutes. I'm coming up from Hollow's Lake."

"I'll let everyone know. Dallas is in town this morning so I'll text him the situation. He'll want to meet up with us. The twins are in the barn so they'll be easy to round up. I'm not sure where Colin is, but he'll want to know what's going on and pitch in to help," Austin said.

Joshua, the youngest twin, had been traveling back and forth to his job in Colorado. He'd been having the most difficult time with the transition to rancher, given that he loved his job in law enforcement. Tyler was glad to have the extra help. He thanked his brother even though he knew Austin wouldn't see it as necessary. "I'll see you in a few."

"We're all here for you. Just let us know what you need and we'll make it happen," Austin said. "In the meantime, I'll watch your back as you enter from the south end of the property."

Tyler ended the call with the push of a button on his steering wheel. Red didn't immediately speak.

She finally leaned forward and said, "I didn't know there were twins in your family."

It was a distraction from the helplessness they both felt being in the SUV driving home rather than being there to save her sister.

"The youngest boys, Ryder and Joshua," he said.

"Now I get why you seem to understand

twins so well," she said with a hollow quality in her voice. She was talking, going through the motions, but her heart wasn't in the conversation.

He understood. Sometimes people needed to do something to keep busy or they'd go crazy. Given the current situation, Red had every right to be distant. And he had another bomb to drop on her. "Tommy's going to be at the cabin when we arrive."

Red shot a look at him.

"I didn't tell him anything. I said that I wouldn't go behind your back and I didn't. But he has to be involved now. He has resources that can help find your sister."

She started to put up more of a fight but seemed to lose steam as she blew out a defeated-sounding sigh.

"Whatever it takes to get my sister back alive," she said quietly. "I'll do anything to make sure she's safe."

JESSICA COULD BARELY BREATHE. Ever since she'd heard the news about her sister it felt as if the air had thinned and the walls were closing in on her. If Milton had gotten to her, and it had to be him, then Jenn was as good as dead. The man had a violent background and nothing to lose. There would be no incentive to keep Jenn alive if she didn't cooperate.

Based on her sister's condition, Jessica wasn't sure if her sister would be coherent enough to say where the necklace was even if she did know.

And what if she knew exactly where the necklace was? What if she'd figured it out? If she told Milton, he'd kill her and dump the body just as ruthlessly as he'd tried before.

"You said you were going to take care of my parents."

"They're on a ranch in Montana," Tyler said.

"My dad's always wanted to go fly-fishing," she said wistfully, trying to absorb all the information coming at her.

"That's how we convinced him to leave. Also, he thinks his daughters are joining him there for Thanksgiving."

"Does he know about all this? He and mother will be so worried," she said.

"Thinks you two arranged the trip with the caveat they had to leave immediately," Tyler said, and there was a sad quality to his tone.

"I'm more than happy to reimburse you for the expenses," she offered.

"It's not that. He sounds like a decent man and I hated lying to him," he said.

Their worlds had never felt so different. She

and her sister were running from the law while Tyler's best friend was the sheriff. He was a good person who stepped in to help when most would run the other way. Would she do the same for a stranger? She liked to think she would, but then she'd never been asked to dodge bullets for anyone before.

But that was for her blood, her sister. No matter how crazy things got, Tyler stayed the course and offered his life to help. She thought about how much she'd been asking of him, forcing an honest man to lie to the people he loved, and a hard knot formed in her stomach.

"You can take me to the sheriff's office to file a report and leave me there. You've done enough for my family," she started, but his hand came off the steering wheel long enough to stop her.

"Don't push me away." His fingers closed around hers as he temporarily steered with one hand.

Was she?

"Every time we get close, you tell me to leave," he continued. "There's only one thing you need to know about a Texan—we don't quit when life gets tough."

Those words, his support, wrapped around her, bathing her in warmth. She couldn't deny his point. Every time they got close and she started opening up, she found a reason to shut down. He'd never left her side. "I don't know how to let go of the feeling that you're going to walk away at some point."

"I can't promise forever, but I do know that I've never felt like this about anyone before," he said.

"Me, too. That's exactly what I'm afraid of."

"Can you take a step back once we get Jenn back and life returns to normal and see where this leads?" he asked as he pulled into an area that finally looked familiar.

"I don't know," was all she could say. He deserved the truth.

"Do me a favor," he said.

"If I can."

"Don't make any decisions right now." He pulled into the garage, turned off the engine and held on to the key. He didn't make a move to get out of the SUV. "Not while everything's turned upside down."

For her own protection, she needed to tell him that was impossible. That she'd already made her choice…to go home and try to forget everything that had happened these past few days. And yet it would be impossible not to remember last night.

Before he could say anything to change her

mind, Jessica opened the door and stepped out of the SUV.

They came from two different worlds, knew very little about each other, and trying to convince herself they could somehow magically make it all work would be foolish.

"The door's unlocked," he said, moving from the driver's side.

She walked in and forced her thoughts away from the feeling that this was home. It wasn't home. Home was with her parents in Shreveport.

He grabbed her elbow as she crossed into the kitchen, spun her around and pinned her against the wall.

"I get that you've lost a lot and that you're scared. But give us a chance." His steady gaze, those dark eyes—she could lose all sense of time. Even forget how messed up her life was right then.

The doorbell rang.

He didn't move and she didn't speak.

"I'll take that to mean you're at least thinking about what I said."

She looked away. No way could she look into those eyes any longer with what she was prepared to do.

An urgent knock sounded at the front door. No doubt it was the sheriff. She'd most likely be arrested for lying to an officer of the law. Would Tyler still want to have anything to do with her then? He wasn't thinking clearly.

He kissed her anyway, slow and sweet. She molded against him.

"Tyler, I saw you drive in," the sheriff said through the door.

Tyler pressed his forehead to hers and closed his eyes.

The next thing she knew, he'd gone into the other room and opened the door. The sheriff walked in first, followed by three men who looked related to Tyler, and a woman.

"I'm Stacy," she said, offering a hand.

Jessica took it and then the tears came.

Stacy pulled her into a hug. "It's going to be okay, you hear me? These men will find your sister and bring her back safe and sound. They're good men and they'll look out for you."

Those words were soothing, and a sense of calm radiated from Stacy.

"Thank you," Jessica said softly. She took a fortifying breath and straightened her shoulders.

Thankfully, the men had moved into the kitchen, gathering around the granite island and passing out mugs of coffee.

"These are my brothers, Austin, Ryder and Joshua," Tyler said.

"Dallas is on his way and Colin must be out of cell range," one of the men said. She recognized the voice as the one on the phone, so he had to be Austin.

"Nice to meet everyone." Each shook her hand and it was easy to guess who the twins were based on the fact that they looked so much alike.

They huddled around the coffeepot as Tyler moved to her side and took her hand.

No one made her feel the way Tyler did. And a big part of her didn't feel worthy of that kind of love. Wow. Was that why she took care of everyone around her? She didn't feel like she deserved real love?

Before she could talk herself out of holding Tyler's hand, he put his arm around her and she leaned into his strength. It was time to bite the bullet and own up to her fraudulence. "I haven't been completely honest with you, sheriff. My name is Jessica and I've been covering for my twin sister, Jennifer."

"I know," Tommy said, and she almost thought she didn't hear him correctly. She must've shot him one wild look because he put his hand up. "I didn't at first, but I started piecing things together and when I dug into your sister's background and found you everything snapped into place."

"I understand if you need to arrest me or something," she said. "But I'd appreciate it if you let me help find my sister first."

The sheriff made a face. "Arrest you? For what? Being a witness to a crime?"

Tyler squeezed her and she'd never felt more safe in someone's arms. But her sister was out there with a crazed man who had nothing to lose.

"Tell us what you know," Tyler said to the sheriff.

"We've been able to ascertain that James Milton owes Randall Beauchamp a large sum of money. His interest in the Infinity Sapphire is twofold—clear his debt and get enough money to start fresh somewhere else. He's been studying for a real estate license in Nevada, so my guess is that he's been planning his exit from Baton Rouge for a while."

"So, we know that he's involved and that Jenn was set up. Why does everyone think she knows where the necklace is?" Tyler asked.

"Because she does," Jessica said. "She might not even know it, but she does. It's the only thing that makes sense."

"What do you mean?" Tyler asked, clearly confused.

A picture was finally emerging. "Jenn said that Milton kept asking about the box. Maybe

Ashton asked her hide something for him but she may not have known what it was."

"It would also mean that she trusted the person who gave it to her," Tyler said. "And we already know she was having an affair with Ashton."

One of the brothers set up a laptop on one side of the island and plugged in a thumb drive. "This is the footage from the hospital."

It was grainy, just as they'd been told, but it was so obvious that the person walking out was not James Milton. "That's Ashton Brasseux."

"How can it be? He and his wife, Emma-Kate were kidnapped," Tyler said, and then it dawned on him. "Or so he wanted everyone to think."

Jessica sipped from the mug she'd been handed earlier.

"Local police did some digging and found out that the Brasseuxs were having a little money trouble. Ashton and Emma-Kate were separating and she believed that he was seeing someone else," the sheriff said.

"My sister," Jessica said quietly. Jessica turned her full attention to the sheriff. "I know how this looks. All evidence points to Jenn taking the sapphire or at the very least being involved in stealing and hiding it. Other people seem to believe the same thing, bad people, but I know in my heart that my sister would never do that. She was in love with Ashton Brasseux and he set her up."

"I have to follow the evidence," the sheriff said. "But I promise to look at all the facts and keep an open mind."

She smiled, nodded. Under the circumstances, he was being generous. "Thank you."

"What's our next step?" Tyler asked. "We know that Jenn is in danger and we need to find her."

Tommy nodded.

"Do you know anything about the person who has been asking around for me?" Tyler asked.

"I tracked him down and he was an investigator for the Brasseux's insurance company," the sheriff said. "We just need to make sure he stays out of the way."

"Any chance that necklace is here on the property?" Tyler asked.

The doorbell rang.

Tyler excused himself and answered the door. "Janis, come in."

"I brought food," she said, carrying a full basket of muffins and pastries.

"Let me take that," he said, and she seemed to know better than to argue.

Janis followed Tyler into the kitchen. Her gaze moved around the island, stopping on Jessica.

"Good morning, Mrs. Templeton," Janis said. "I didn't know you were here."

Jessica shot Tyler a look. "I'm sorry, have we met?"

Janis stared, openmouthed. "You were here a couple of weeks ago with your husband."

"I'm afraid that I have no idea what you're talking about," Jessica said, but the light went on at the same time Austin turned the laptop around.

"Who'd she come with?" Austin asked.

"Her husband," Janis said, confusion knitting her eyebrows. "But I must be mistaken."

"Does Mr. Templeton look like this?" Austin asked, angling the screen toward Janis.

"Why, yes. It's a little blurry but that's him," she said emphatically.

"Which means that Jenn and Ashton came here, and Milton must've known she would come back to a place where they'd already been," Tyler said, and the sheriff nodded.

Tyler poured another cup of coffee. "Do you remember any details about their booking?"

"It's been a couple of weeks. Let me think," Janis said as he handed her a mug.

Hope blossomed for the first time since this

whole ordeal started. If Jenn had been taken by Ashton, surely she'd be safe. If he loved her, he wouldn't do anything bad to her. Would he?

The man stole a family heirloom from his wife and gave it to his mistress to hide, promising her they'd be together forever. The short-lived burst of hope immediately died.

"If he gets the necklace, he'll hurt her," Jessica said. "We have to find them first."

"IS THERE ANYTHING specific you remember about the couple?" Tyler asked Janis.

"They stayed in their room most of the time. Didn't book a hunting trip, I remember that for sure because I thought it was odd this time of year," Janis said. "I remembered thinking that they must be honeymooners."

Reality hit Tyler harder than a ton of bricks. "She hid the necklace in the main house."

The sound of bar stools scraping across tile echoed as everyone stood at the same time.

"I can check the registry and tell you which room they stayed in," Janis offered, and they were already making a move toward the door.

"We'll tear the place apart if we have to," Austin said.

As soon as the group left, Jessica said, "They won't be on the property. We might find the necklace, but with security here he's not stupid enough to risk coming straight at us. He'll take her somewhere else until he comes up with a plan."

"First, let's get the necklace. That's the best thing we can do to ensure your sister's safety. He won't do anything to her if he thinks she's useful."

She followed Tyler to the garage where he fired up the SUV and backed out.

The drive to the main house took ten minutes. Denali was on the front porch waiting.

"Hey, buddy," Tyler said as the chocolate lab trotted over to greet him.

"I'll just check the registry," Janis said.

The main house was set back, but they could see the road from the porch. An older model, white four-door Mazda pulled up in front of the gate, someone was pushed out and the car sped off.

"It's her," Jessica shouted. "It's Jenn."

Chapter Seventeen

Tyler darted toward Jenn as the guards in the shack bolted outside. "She's clear. She's with us."

Most of the house emptied, with all the boys running close behind Jessica, and she had never felt so protected and secure in her life.

"Jenn," she said as she dropped down beside her sister, who was folded onto her side. She wore a jacket over her shirt, which was odd considering the weather had warmed up.

"Go," Jenn whispered, looking too weak to move. She made a grunting noise before repeating the word.

Sheriff Tommy knelt next to Jenn, his gaze sweeping over her. "Everyone back away."

"I'm not going anywhere," Jessica said, just as she noticed sweat beads on Jenn's forehead. She wiped them away. "It's okay. I'm here now and I won't let those men hurt you."

Jenn winced as she shook her head. "Go."

Her sister was weak and clearly not thinking straight. Jessica had no idea what those jerks had done to her sister but she hoped they rotted in jail for their crimes. She vaguely heard the sheriff in the background giving a description of the vehicle that had sped away.

"Everyone needs to step away," he said, unzipping Jenn's jacket to reveal a bomb strapped to her body.

Tears fell freely as Jessica held on to her sister's hand. "I'm not leaving you."

There was a piece of white paper sticking out of her jacket pocket. Jenn angled her head toward it.

"Sheriff—" Jessica started but was cut off.

"I see it. Everyone needs to get back," the sheriff demanded, leaving no room for doubt that he was serious.

The brothers did as instructed, except for Tyler. He didn't budge.

"I have protocol to follow, Tyler," the sheriff said.

"And I have my loyalties," Tyler retorted.

"If you're not going to make this easy, then scoot over so I can take a closer look," the sheriff said. He took out a pair of something that looked like tweezers and put on rubber gloves. He removed the folded piece of paper and peeled it open.

"It's easy. We get the necklace or she goes boom. You have one hour to leave it where you found her sister. No cops."

"He used the term *we*," the sheriff said. "We're dealing with a network."

"Which one of these guys has experience with explosives?" Tyler said.

"Chemical engineer," Jenn managed to say. "Ashton."

Everyone reacted to the news.

"She needs medical help." Jessica fought back tears as she whispered reassurances to Jenn.

The sheriff leaned back on his heels and evaluated the situation. "Ashton must be our guy. He's in charge."

Heads bobbed in agreement.

Tyler glanced up at his brothers and shooed them back into the house to search for the piece of jewelry.

"They must think we already have the necklace," Tyler said. "We'd have to hightail it to drive to Diablo's Rock in an hour. I can get there on Digby in forty-five minutes."

"Someone needs to show up whether we have the necklace or not," the sheriff said. "It'll be our best chance to nab them."

"They'll be watching for police," Jessica said. "We mess this up and they'll push the button."

"They can do that anyway once they get the necklace," Tyler warned, and he was right.

"This looks like pretty standard material." The sheriff rattled off names that didn't mean much to Jessica, then said, "They'd have to be using a wireless trigger mechanism."

"Cell phone," Jenn said through a coughing fit.

Both the sheriff and Tyler stiffened until she calmed again.

"So, if they need a wireless connection to detonate the bomb, then what happens if I take her out of cell range?" Tyler asked. "There are so many dead spots on the property, it would be easy to take her somewhere there's no signal. In fact, Diablo's Rock is a dead zone."

"We need to be careful moving her," the sheriff said.

"I'll get the SUV," Tyler said as Austin burst out the front door.

"Found it stuffed between the mattresses," he said, holding out the Infinity Sapphire. The brilliant stones caught the light just right, leaving sparkly streaks in the air.

"You're going to be okay," Jessica soothed, brushing Jenn's hair from her face. "You're here and we're not going to let anything happen to you."

"So stupid," Jenn managed to say. "Thought he loved me."

"I know, sweetie," Jessica said. "But he's not good enough for you. And we're going to make sure he spends the rest of his life in jail."

Jenn nodded and a tear streaked her cheek.

"Move her carefully," the sheriff said as Tyler moved to the other side of Jenn.

"You might want to step behind the SUV," Tyler said to Jessica, but she was already shaking her head.

"I'm staying right here by my sister," Jessica said. She expected Tyler to put up an argument but he nodded and kept going, gently moving Jenn into the back of the SUV on top of layers of sleeping bags.

"I'll need you with me," Tyler said.

She moved to the passenger side as soon as Jenn was secure. "I have no plans to leave her."

"I was afraid you'd say that."

"WE HAVE TO approach the same way you did with the ATVs," Tyler said to Jessica as he parked the SUV a few yards from the rock. Her body language screamed fear. No doubt she remembered the last time she'd been there a few days ago.

His brothers were near, they'd fanned out around the area, but there was no cell coverage out there. Good for Jenn but bad for overall communication.

"Stay here," he said, handing her the Sig Sauer she'd used before. "Don't let on that anyone's in the back of the SUV. Don't even glance back there, okay?"

"I'm good." She palmed the weapon and then double-checked the chamber.

"Remind me not to get on your bad side later." He kissed her. "I need to check the area. The boys aren't far and they know how to hide. The tricky part will be communicating with them if we get in trouble."

"We're going to be fine. We have to be."

She didn't say that their lives depended on it but they did.

Tyler moved to the rock and dug his boots in, moving to high ground to get a better look at the area. As he crested the rock he thought about how much his life had changed since the last time he was there. Everything had been turned upside down, he'd never been in more danger and never been more in love. The danger part he could handle.

He saw the glint of metal coming behind a bush on the east side just as the telltale flash of fire followed. The bullet pierced him. Shock registered as he missed his footing and tumbled the forty-foot drop from Diablo's peak.

JESSICA HEARD A gun fire. She bolted from the SUV in time to see Tyler tumbling down the face of the rock. Panic engulfed her and her pulse skyrocketed. Before she had a chance to rationalize her actions she was running toward him.

Please let him be okay.

Her stomach twisted as she got close enough to see him lying there, facedown, unmoving. All she could think about was getting to him and then she saw the blood through his plaid shirt.

There was no way to contact his brothers. Her own sister lay in the SUV, unconscious. All Jessica's hopes had been riding on the cowboy and now he was dying, leaving her, too. It was a selfish thought and she knew it. She tamped it down and spun around to the sound of footsteps running up behind her. There were three men, all with weapons pointed directly at her chest. She pointed her own gun at the ringleader, Ashton. "Stop or I'll shoot."

"Whoa," he said to the others, holding his hands out for them to stay behind.

They were out of cell phone range. Tyler's

brothers had to have heard the shot, hadn't they? And all of them were about to die.

Well, she planned on taking a couple of these jerks with her.

"Back off if you want the necklace," she said, taking a step away as the men slowed their approach.

"You don't have a play here, honey," Milton said, and her skin crawled at the sound of his voice.

She retreated a few more steps until her back hit a solid wall of rock. "Don't come any closer or I'll start shooting."

All three men stopped. The third fit the description of the man in the suit who'd been asking around for Tyler. It dawned on Jessica. The insurance adjuster must be in on it. Milton wasn't working for Beauchamp, he was in league with Ashton.

"How did they talk you into joining them?" she asked the third man.

"This guy?" A wide smile broke on Ashton's face. "Fraternity brothers forever."

He and Ashton were friends? He must've been offered a cut.

"My sister thought you loved her," she said as Ashton took another menacing step toward her. Anger burned through her chest. She hated the guy, but could she kill someone?

It was either kill or be killed.

Ashton ignored her comment and made a move to kick Tyler. "How'd this jerk get involved?"

Jessica closed her eyes and pulled the trigger. By the time she opened them a second later, chaos had broken out.

Ashton was on the ground, wrestling with Tyler, who had already shot Milton. She'd nicked the insurance guy who was diving on top of Tyler and Ashton.

Milton didn't seem to realize he'd been shot because he lunged toward her.

"Bitch," he said as he dived.

She whirled to the right and he smacked into the rock, shoulder first, but managed to knock the gun out of her hand. His thick hand clutched at her until he gained purchase on her shirt. He shoved her to the ground and she desperately felt around for the Sig.

Milton twisted until he was straddled over her. She glanced to the side in time to see that Tyler and Ashton were wrestling for a gun. Ashton's friend was rearing back to deck Tyler.

In a burst, the gun went off and Tyler managed to roll on top of Ashton.

There was so much blood.

Milton raised his hand high and she could see a rock in his palm.

And then she heard the footsteps.

"Put your weapons down," Sheriff Tommy's familiar voice said.

Milton ignored the request. She wiggled but he was too heavy to buck him off. And then another gunshot roared. Milton's eyes bulged after taking the second hit. He slumped to the side allowing Jessica to slide out from underneath him.

Austin wrangled Ashton's friend away, pulling him by the foot. But Tyler and Ashton were too tangled up. A shot was as likely to hit Tyler.

Jessica scooted away from Milton and gentle arms pulled her to her feet. She wasn't sure which one of the twins helped her, but she was grateful.

Tyler pushed Ashton off him and got in a solid punch.

Ashton's head bobbled and then he fell forward, unconscious.

The sheriff was by Tyler's side before she could open her mouth to speak. He zip-cuffed Ashton's hands behind his back.

Jessica ran to Tyler to see just how much blood he'd lost. His brothers were by his side as his eyes closed.

"He's going to be all right, isn't he?" Jessica asked, tears streaking from her eyes. She must've looked as torn on the outside as she

was on the inside. Tyler was bleeding, unconscious. Jenn was alone in that SUV where anyone or anything could get to her.

"Austin is with your sister," the sheriff said,
easing one of her fears as she heard the *whop,
whop, whop* of the helicopter.

Chapter Eighteen

Tyler blinked his eyes open, quickly closing them again. His arm came up to shield them from the bright light shooting daggers through his retinas. His eyes burned as if they'd been branded.

"Hold on there, buddy," Austin said, and the sound of his voice moved toward Tyler until he felt his brother's presence at his side. "Let me get the nurse."

"I'm fine," Tyler blew him off, knowing full well it wasn't the nurse he needed. "Where is she?"

"About that," Austin started.

Tyler's hand came up to stop his brother from delivering bad news. Thinking about losing the woman he'd fallen for hit him like a physical punch. "Never mind. How long have I been out?"

"Just two days," Austin supplied. "And you've been in and out."

"Really?" Tyler needed to get well so he could find Red. There was so much he wanted to say to her. He squinted and a figure in the corner caught his eye.

"Hi, there," Jessica said, moving to his side. She was wringing her hands and that wasn't a good sign.

Austin winked. "I'll leave you two alone to talk."

All the words he'd intended to say died on Tyler's lips when he made eye contact. "How's your sister?"

"Dr. McConnell says Jenn will be fine," Red said, stopping just out of arm's reach. "She's down the hall, already sitting up and chatting. She confirmed that she'd been dating Ashton and he told her that she needed to take care of something to secure their future. He'd said he and his wife were in a loveless marriage and that he'd been planning to leave her for months. He gave her the box and Jenn naively didn't open it. He'd already arranged for Milton to steal it so there'd be a double payoff. His fraternity brother had planned to help him scam the insurance company and was going to get a cut for selling the Infinity Sapphire to Beauchamp's people."

"But Ashton was only using your sister. Setting her up to do the time for the theft," Tyler said, his hands aching to reach out to her, hold her.

"He planned to let her do the time or be killed by Beauchamp. Milton had secretly set up another buyer, and that's who showed at the motel room in Bluff," she said, shifting her weight from her left to right foot. "When Milton didn't produce the necklace, the guy figured he'd been duped. Their whole plan fell apart. Jenn was the only one who knew where the necklace was this whole time. And it turns out we were right that Elijah wanted the necklace to make money off his own sale."

"It can't be easy for Jenn knowing the person she fell in love with was using her," Tyler said.

"Those wounds will be harder to heal," Red admitted. "But just as fast as Jenn falls in love, she can fall out of it."

"And how about you?" he asked. "Do you fall in and out of love quickly?"

She stared at the floor instead of answering.

It was now or never, he thought. "It's finally over. But what happens next? You go back to your life and I do the same? I've never felt this way about anyone before, Jessica. I'm in love with you and I don't want this to be the end."

A little gasp escaped before she suppressed it. "I feel the same way. I've fallen hard for you, Tyler. But it would be crazy to throw away my life and you certainly can't throw away yours. Especially not when neither of us can be certain this isn't a circumstantial romance."

"Do you really believe that's true?" He did his best to mask the hurt in his voice.

"No, of course not. I want to believe this is real, but I need more than a few days to process what's going on between us and make sure it can become something permanent," she said, and there was no covering the confusion in hers.

"Come here," he said and she did.

She eased onto the side of the bed and he put his arms around her. "Let's just agree to keep seeing each other as much as we can until we figure it all out. I don't want to spend another day without you in my life but I'll wait for you."

He brushed a tear off her cheek. "No more crying. This is a good thing. *We're* a good thing."

She leaned into him gently. "Yes, we are. I was so scared when you were shot. I was so afraid of losing you."

"You don't have to," he whispered into her ear and then kissed her neck. "I'm right here."

JESSICA HAD WAITED six agonizing months for this day to come. She finished her breakfast and grabbed her car keys off the counter with giddy anticipation. Now that Jenn had returned to Shreveport and learned to run the family business, Jessica felt comfortable enough to let the employees know there'd be a change in the guard at Davidson Cleaning Services and Jenn would be taking over.

As she walked out the front door, she froze. "Tyler? What are you doing here? We aren't supposed to see each other until this weekend." And she'd been planning to drop the same bomb on him for weeks. She was ready. She knew that their love was real and could last.

"I couldn't wait to see you," he said with a smile.

She took the couple of steps from the porch quickly, ready to share her good news. Before she could reach him, he dropped down on one knee and produced a small velvet box.

"You are the love of my life. When you're not with me I'm empty in a way I've never known before. I want you to spend the rest of your life with me and our children," he said.

Tears were already flowing down Jessica's cheeks, tears of pure joy.

"You want children?" she asked.

"At least four, but I figured I needed to talk

to you about the number before I started making plans," he said. "Jessica, will you marry me?"

She nodded as she wrapped her arms around him. "I love you, Tyler O'Brien, and I can't wait to start our life together."

He kissed her, tenderly at first, but need built quickly.

"Will you come home with me and stay this time?" he asked. "The past six months have been killing me and I don't want to spend another day apart."

"Yes, I'll marry you. And, yes, I'll come home with you. I can't imagine a better place to bring up our kids," she said. "And you know what? I was just on my way to let the employees know that my sister is taking over."

"Good. Because when you come home with me this time, I'm not letting you go."

"You can hold on to me forever," she said. And she couldn't wait to spend the rest of her life with her Texas cowboy.

* * * * *

USA TODAY bestselling author Barb Han's miniseries, CATTLEMEN CRIME CLUB, *continues soon. Look for it wherever Harlequin Intrigue books are sold!*

LARGER-PRINT BOOKS!

◆HARLEQUIN

Presents®

PASSION
GUARANTEED
SEDUCTION

GET 2 FREE LARGER-PRINT NOVELS PLUS 2 FREE GIFTS!

YES! Please send me 2 FREE LARGER-PRINT Harlequin Presents® novels and my 2 FREE gifts (gifts are worth about $10). After receiving them, if I don't wish to receive any more books, I can return the shipping statement marked "cancel." If I don't cancel, I will receive 6 brand-new novels every month and be billed just $5.30 per book in the U.S. or $5.74 per book in Canada. That's a saving of at least 12% off the cover price! It's quite a bargain! Shipping and handling is just 50¢ per book in the U.S. and 75¢ per book in Canada.* I understand that accepting the 2 free books and gifts places me under no obligation to buy anything. I can always return a shipment and cancel at any time. Even if I never buy another book, the two free books and gifts are mine to keep forever.

176/376 HDN GHVY

Name	(PLEASE PRINT)	
Address		Apt. #
City	State/Prov.	Zip/Postal Code

Signature (if under 18, a parent or guardian must sign)

Mail to the **Reader Service:**
IN U.S.A.: P.O. Box 1867, Buffalo, NY 14240-1867
IN CANADA: P.O. Box 609, Fort Erie, Ontario L2A 5X3

**Are you a subscriber to Harlequin Presents® books
and want to receive the larger-print edition?
Call 1-800-873-8635 today or visit us at www.ReaderService.com.**

* Terms and prices subject to change without notice. Prices do not include applicable taxes. Sales tax applicable in N.Y. Canadian residents will be charged applicable taxes. Offer not valid in Quebec. This offer is limited to one order per household. Not valid for current subscribers to Harlequin Presents Larger-Print books. All orders subject to credit approval. Credit or debit balances in a customer's account(s) may be offset by any other outstanding balance owed by or to the customer. Please allow 4 to 6 weeks for delivery. Offer available while quantities last.

Your Privacy—The Reader Service is committed to protecting your privacy. Our Privacy Policy is available online at www.ReaderService.com or upon request from the Reader Service.

We make a portion of our mailing list available to reputable third parties that offer products we believe may interest you. If you prefer that we not exchange your name with third parties, or if you wish to clarify or modify your communication preferences, please visit us at www.ReaderService.com/consumerschoice or write to us at Reader Service Preference Service, P.O. Box 9062, Buffalo, NY 14240-9062. Include your complete name and address.

HPLP15

LARGER-PRINT BOOKS!

GET 2 FREE LARGER-PRINT NOVELS PLUS
2 FREE GIFTS!

H HARLEQUIN®

Romance

From the Heart, For the Heart

YES! Please send me 2 FREE LARGER-PRINT Harlequin® Romance novels and my 2 FREE gifts (gifts are worth about $10). After receiving them, if I don't wish to receive any more books, I can return the shipping statement marked "cancel." If I don't cancel, I will receive 4 brand-new novels every month and be billed just $5.09 per book in the U.S. or $5.49 per book in Canada. That's a savings of at least 15% off the cover price! It's quite a bargain! Shipping and handling is just 50¢ per book in the U.S. and 75¢ per book in Canada.* I understand that accepting the 2 free books and gifts places me under no obligation to buy anything. I can always return a shipment and cancel at any time. Even if I never buy another book, the two free books and gifts are mine to keep forever.

119/319 HDN GHWC

Name	(PLEASE PRINT)

Address	Apt. #

City	State/Prov.	Zip/Postal Code

Signature (if under 18, a parent or guardian must sign)

Mail to the **Reader Service:**
IN U.S.A.: P.O. Box 1867, Buffalo, NY 14240-1867
IN CANADA: P.O. Box 609, Fort Erie, Ontario L2A 5X3

Want to try two free books from another line?
Call 1-800-873-8635 or visit www.ReaderService.com.

* Terms and prices subject to change without notice. Prices do not include applicable taxes. Sales tax applicable in N.Y. Canadian residents will be charged applicable taxes. Offer not valid in Quebec. This offer is limited to one order per household. Not valid for current subscribers to Harlequin Romance Larger-Print books. All orders subject to credit approval. Credit or debit balances in a customer's account(s) may be offset by any other outstanding balance owed by or to the customer. Please allow 4 to 6 weeks for delivery. Offer available while quantities last.

Your Privacy—The Reader Service is committed to protecting your privacy. Our Privacy Policy is available online at www.ReaderService.com or upon request from the Reader Service.

We make a portion of our mailing list available to reputable third parties that offer products we believe may interest you. If you prefer that we not exchange your name with third parties, or if you wish to clarify or modify your communication preferences, please visit us at www.ReaderService.com/consumerchoice or write to us at Reader Service Preference Service, P.O. Box 9062, Buffalo, NY 14240-9062. Include your complete name and address.

HRLP15

LARGER-PRINT BOOKS!
GET 2 FREE LARGER-PRINT NOVELS PLUS
2 FREE GIFTS!

HARLEQUIN

super romance

More Story...More Romance

WESTERN **WP** PROMISES

YES! Please send me **The Western Promises Collection** in Larger Print. This collection begins with 3 FREE books and 2 FREE gifts (gifts valued at approx. $14.00 retail) in the first shipment, along with the other first 4 books from the collection! If I do not cancel, I will receive 8 monthly shipments until I have the entire 51-book Western Promises collection. I will receive 2 or 3 FREE books in each shipment and I will pay just $4.99 US/ $5.89 CDN for each of the other four books in each shipment, plus $2.99 for shipping and handling per shipment. *If I decide to keep the entire collection, I'll have paid for only 32 books, because 19 books are FREE! I understand that accepting the 3 free books and gifts places me under no obligation to buy anything. I can always return a shipment and cancel at any time. My free books and gifts are mine to keep no matter what I decide.

272 HCN 3070 472 HCN 3070

Name _____ (PLEASE PRINT) _____

Address _____ Apt. # _____

City _____ State/Prov. _____ Zip/Postal Code _____

Signature (if under 18, a parent or guardian must sign)

Mail to the **Reader Service:**
IN U.S.A.: P.O. Box 1867, Buffalo, NY 14240-1867
IN CANADA: P.O. Box 609, Fort Erie, Ontario L2A 5X3

* Terms and prices subject to change without notice. Prices do not include applicable taxes. Sales tax applicable in N.Y. Canadian residents will be charged applicable taxes. This offer is limited to one order per household. All orders subject to approval. Credit or debit balances in a customer's account(s) may be offset by any other outstanding balance owed by or to the customer. Please allow 4 to 6 weeks for delivery. Offer available while quantities last. Offer not available to Quebec residents.

Your Privacy—The Reader Service is committed to protecting your privacy. Our Privacy Policy is available online at www.ReaderService.com or upon request from the Reader Service.

We make a portion of our mailing list available to reputable third parties that offer products we believe may interest you. If you prefer that we not exchange your name with third parties, or if you wish to clarify or modify your communication preferences, please visit us at www.ReaderService.com/consumerchoice or write to us at Reader Service Preference Service, P.O. Box 9062, Buffalo, N.Y. 14240-9062. Include your complete name and address.

WPBPA16R